CHOKE ME

A K&K KINKY READS COLLECTION NOVELLA

KER DUKEY

K WEBSTER

K&K
KINKY READS

CHOKE *Me*

A K&K Kinky Reads Collection Novella

By

Ker Dukey and K Webster

COPYRIGHT

Cover Design: All by Design
Photo: Adobe Stock
Editor: Emily A. Lawrence

Me

BLURB

I had a plan.
Make Ren Hayes pay.
But plans don't always turn out the way we want them to.

He was found not guilty of murdering my best friend.
But that doesn't make him innocent.
In my eyes, he's guilty.

Guilty of charming everyone around him into believing his innocence.
Guilty of being so intoxicating I forget who he is—what he is.
And guilty of awakening parts of me I never knew existed before his touch.

I know eventually, I'll succumb.

His allure beckons me.
Keeping me on the edge of madness between lust and hate.

In the end, it's me who's guilty.
Guilty of allowing him to take my breath away.

Books By Ker Dukey

BOOKS BY KER DUKEY

Empathy Series:

Empathy

Desolate

Vacant – Novella

Deadly – Novella

The Broken Series:

The Broken

The Broken Parts of Us

The Broken Tethers That Bind Us – Novella

The Broken Forever – Novella

The Men by Numbers Series:

Ten

Six

Drawn to You Duet:

Drawn to You

Lines Drawn

Standalone Novels:

My Soul Keeper

Lost

I See You

The Beats in Rift

Devil

Co-Written with D. Sidebottom

The Deception Series:

FaCade

Cadence

Beneath Innocence – Novella

The Lilith's Army MC Series:

Taking Avery

Finding Rhiannon

Coming Home TBA

Co-Written with K Webster

The Pretty Little Dolls Series:

Pretty Stolen Dolls

Pretty Lost Dolls

Pretty New Doll

Pretty Broken Dolls

The V Games Series:

Vlad

Ven

Vas

KKinky Reads Collection:

Share Me

Choke Me

Joint Series

Four Fathers Series:

Blackstone by J.D. Hollyfield

Kingston by Dani René

Pearson by K Webster

Wheeler by Ker Dukey

Four Sons Series:

Nixon by Ker Dukey

Hayden by J.D Hollyfield

Brock by Dani René

Camden by K Webster

The Elite Seven Series:

Lust – Ker Dukey

Pride – J.D. Hollyfield

Wrath – Claire C. Riley

Envy – M.N.Forgy

Gluttony – K Webster

Sloth – Giana Darling

Greed – Ker Dukey & K Webster

Books By K Webster

BOOKS BY K WEBSTER

Psychological Romance Standalones:

My Torin

Whispers and the Roars

Cold Cole Heart

Blue Hill Blood

Romantic Suspense Standalones:

Dirty Ugly Toy

El Malo

Notice

Sweet Jayne

The Road Back to Us

Surviving Harley

Love and Law

Moth to a Flame

Erased

Extremely Forbidden Romance Standalones:

The Wild

Hale

Like Dragonflies

Taboo Treats:

Bad Bad Bad

Coach Long

Ex-Rated Attraction

Mr. Blakely

Easton

Crybaby

Lawn Boys

Malfeasance

Renner's Rules

The Glue

Dane

Enzo

Red Hot Winter

KKinky Reads Collection:

Share Me

Choke Me

Contemporary Romance Standalones:

The Day She Cried

Untimely You

Heath

Sundays are for Hangovers

A Merry Christmas with Judy

Zeke's Eden

Schooled by a Senior

Give Me Yesterday

Sunshine and the Stalker

Bidding for Keeps

B-Sides and Rarities

Paranormal Romance Standalones:

Apartment 2B

Running Free

Mad Sea

War & Peace Series:

This is War, Baby (Book 1)

This is Love, Baby (Book 2)

This Isn't Over, Baby (Book 3)

This Isn't You, Baby (Book 4)

This is Me, Baby (Book 5)

This Isn't Fair, Baby (Book 6)

This is the End, Baby (Book 7 – a novella)

Lost Planet Series:

The Forgotten Commander (Book 1)

The Vanished Specialist (Book 2)

2 Lovers Series:

Text 2 Lovers (Book 1)

Hate 2 Lovers (Book 2)

Thieves 2 Lovers (Book 3)

Pretty Little Dolls Series:

Pretty Stolen Dolls (Book 1)

Pretty Lost Dolls (Book 2)

Pretty New Doll (Book 3)

Pretty Broken Dolls (Book 4)

The V Games Series:

Vlad (Book 1)

Ven (Book 2)

Vas (Book 3)

Four Fathers Books:

Pearson

Four Sons Books:

Camden

Elite Seven Books:

Gluttony

Not Safe for Amazon Books:

The Wild

Hale

Bad Bad Bad

This is War, Baby

Like Dragonflies

The Breaking the Rules Series:

Broken (Book 1)

Wrong (Book 2)

Scarred (Book 3)

Mistake (Book 4)

Crushed (Book 5 – a novella)

The Vegas Aces Series:

Rock Country (Book 1)

Rock Heart (Book 2)

Rock Bottom (Book 3)

The Becoming Her Series:

Becoming Lady Thomas (Book 1)

Becoming Countess Dumont (Book 2)

Becoming Mrs. Benedict (Book 3)

Alpha & Omega Duet:

Alpha & Omega (Book 1)

Omega & Love (Book 2)

Me

AUTHOR NOTE

Breathplay

Erotic asphyxiation, or breathplay, is a sexual practice involving the intentional deprivation of oxygen to the brain by choking, hanging, or other.

Sex always comes with some form of risk. Breathplay, however, and other practices of kink carry an inherent risk. When indulging in breathplay, you should be aware of the emotional and physical dangers on top of the common risks associated with sex.

These sexual activities push limits and should always be practiced safely.

There are two mantras used in the world of BDSM that can help keep you in the territory of healthy sex:

Safe, Sane, and Consensual (SSC).
And Risk Aware Consensual Kink (RACK).

These are the foundation stones of healthy scening.
When engaging in sexual acts with a partner, it's
crucial to keep communication open.
Trust is paramount.

Stay safe.
Stay aware.
Stay satisfied.

CHOKE Me

For our kinky bitches…

Who like the kind of sex that leaves a mark.

ONE

REN

They say blondes have more fun. I always thought that was true. I mean, I'm kind of an expert. Blondes really turn me the fuck on. And the one on her knees, sucking me off like it's her job, she's having a lot of fun. In fact, pretty much all blondes I have ever known have always had fun when it comes to me.

Except one.

As the enthusiastic blonde with her tits hanging out of her dress gags on my dick, my eyes track the unhappy blonde. The annoyed blonde. The blonde who wouldn't know fun if it slapped her in her face with its dick. While I should look away from the scowling blonde to focus on my slobbering blonde, I can't.

I've been looking at her since the day I saw her in the courtroom.

Fuck. It's been ages. Nearly six months now. I stood on trial in front of a jury while the state attempted to prosecute me for the murder of Kate Rose.

"That thing is dangerous," the blonde between my legs mutters breathily before licking the silver ball on the underside of my piercing. "I nearly chipped a tooth."

I drag my eyes from the glaring blonde, who thinks she's hiding in the shadows, to the one smiling at me. "If my dick was in your throat, Tammy, you wouldn't have to worry about those pretty teeth."

Tammy, whom I only met thirty minutes ago, giggles. Her blue eyes are slightly widened as though she's surprised I remembered her name. I remember everyone's name. It's what makes me good at my job. I'm an artist and repertoire rep. I go to bars and clubs, find the really fucking amazing talent, and I sign them to Harose Records. My older brother

Ronan may be the suit who manages the financial end of things, but it's my careful selection and eye for really fucking awesome musicians that keeps the money in his greedy hands in the first place. As much as Ronan likes to play the big-time record exec role, we both know who keeps Harose in fucking business.

I groan when Tammy starts sucking on me again. While she's distracted, I seek out *her*. The fussy blonde. The nosey one. The angry one. As soon as my eyes latch onto her fierce green ones—eyes I only know the color of because I stared at her while on the witness stand—she dips her head down, hiding behind her thick golden locks.

Can't hide from me, nerdy Natasha. I fucking see you.

She may be a nerd on the outside, but she's not fooling anyone. Behind her college sweatshirt are full tits that strain against the material. Her jeans are fitted, molding perfectly to her luscious curves. And the thick, black-rimmed glasses? She may need them to see, but they only serve to make her look hotter. Nerds don't have juicy goddamn lips meant for sucking dick like Natasha does.

As Tammy works my dick over, I can't help but think of the trial. How Natasha Washington stared at me with every ounce of hate she could muster. It was her best friend and roomie who died. Kate Rose was strangled to death. And I was arrested for that shit because my fingerprints were all over the scarf found wrapped around her pretty neck.

We weren't fucking dating, but I had to convince a jury otherwise or spend the next ten to twenty-five years behind bars. I'm too pretty for prison.

Kate was into the same kinks I'm into. It's how we fucking met. She was a gasper, and her death was unfortunate. It will stay with me forever, haunting my choices.

But you can't go to prison for a little breathplay gone wrong.

My attention is dragged back to Tammy. Poor Tammy. Pushing forty, fighting wrinkles, and desperately looking for a successful man like me to get her off her knees once and for all. I stroke her hair as she takes me deep in her throat, pulling out all her tricks. She'll find someone one day, but it sure as hell won't be me. I'm just an asshole who likes his dick sucked.

Natasha's eyes burn into me and I'm once again hunting her down. She's walked out from the shadowed corner, her pouty lips pressed into a firm line. I can practically feel her prissy disappointment rippling over to me. If she'd let me, I'd pull that stick out of her ass real quick and replace it with my cock.

Images of her bent over the sofa she stands behind, my fingers digging into her pale hips, has me coming without warning. Tammy—God love her—swallows down my release like a champ. I grunt, slightly thrusting my hips, as I smirk at Natasha.

Lifting a brow at her, I flash her a smug grin that says, *"You want to be next?"*

Her nostrils flare in disgust.

"What are you doing later?" Tammy asks as she pulls the top of her dress up, putting her fake tits back where they should be. "I could go home with you. Show you a little more of what I'm good at."

I toy with her bleached hair. *Tammy, Tammy, Tammy. You try so hard.* Instead of telling her what's on my mind, I grin at her. "As enticing as that offer is, beautiful, I have to work. I'm on a short break, but I need to get in there to listen to Soul Prison."

She pouts as she stands. I give her ass a little swat before tucking my wet dick in my jeans.

"The night's still young," I tell her. "I saw a couple of suits who look sorely out of place. Maybe you should give them a warm Tammy welcome."

She laughs. "You're an asshole, handsome."

"Never claimed not to be one."

As she sashays away, hot on the prowl for a new mark, I stand and seek out Natasha. Several men stand nearby, their obvious interest in her making her uncomfortable. She's tense and keeps giving them the "back the fuck off" vibes.

Little lamb, you're in the den with the wolves.

I glance at the clock. Fifteen minutes until Soul Prison goes on. Just enough time to see what has dragged Natasha into the VIP room of one of my favorite clubs. I want to see if her face can possibly sour any more while talking to me.

Before I can make my way over to her, my phone buzzes. William Warner's name flashes across the screen. I have half a mind to send it to voicemail, but he'll just bug the shit out of me until I answer. The idiot doesn't have a filter. I can't risk him leaving incriminating shit on my voicemail.

"What?" I grunt out, my eyes once again seeking out Natasha. Her back is turned so that I get a nice view of her curvy ass in her jeans.

"Where are you?" he demands. "I wanted to go out tonight."

William—an old friend from high school who kind of stuck throughout the years despite our vast differences—doesn't mean he wants to go out to party or drink or listen to bands. No, William wants to go out on a hunt for his next bed partner. While he looks okay if you're into a perfect Ken doll look, he lacks the finesse and charm I have. I can grin at any woman, flash her a wink, and lead her to a back room where she'll be all too happy to get a little kinky with me. William is too worried about his public image. He's a sick bastard stuck in a pretty boy's body. Instead of flaunting his darker tastes like I do, he hides them.

"I'm working," I rumble.

I catch Natasha raking her gaze down my front. I'm hard to ignore. Not even Natasha, the little lamb about to get devoured, can ignore me. She hates me—thinks she knows me—but she can't deny the way her body responds around me. It satisfies me to watch her high cheekbones flood with crimson.

"Tomorrow?" William whines. "Please?"

He can't be left alone with his curiosity with kinks. I've already come to his rescue once over that shit. I'll be damned if I do it again. I made the asshole promise not to do anything without my supervision. And because he's somewhat in the public eye, he obeys me, knowing he can't afford to fuck up again.

"We'll see. Gotta go, man." I hang up and run my stare down Natasha's slender throat. It's pale white, desperate to be sucked, marked, and bitten. My dick is hardening again in my jeans at the image of her neck purple and bruised. I have to fist my hand at my side to keep from stalking over to her and pinning her to the wall with my hand around her neck.

I start for her, and for a moment, she seems panicked. She stumbles back a couple of steps until her ass bounces against the wall behind her. A guy nearby laughs and says something to her. Fury causes her brows to crash together. I can practically see the steam coming from her ears. If I can piss her off by simply looking at her, then I can only imagine what sort of response I can get from her when I have her naked and beneath me with my tongue between her thighs.

She brings a shaky hand to her glasses and adjusts them. They were fine, but I remembered this nervous habit from the courtroom. When she was upset or couldn't handle what the prosecutors were saying, she'd absently grab one side of her black glasses with her thin fingers and move her glasses a little. I also know she bites on one corner of her bottom lip when she's about to cry.

She's not biting her lip now.

Now, it's as though she's sharpening her inner claws.

I like pain, little lamb.

Her green eyes glow hot with anger. She's obviously here to confront me. Most likely for being acquitted by the jury. Kate Rose was a nice woman. If they were best friends, Natasha must be fairly nice too for them to get along.

And nice girls don't come after bad boys.

Bad boys will eat nice girls for dinner.

She catches me eyeing her hungrily. I lick my lips and grin at her. I'd give my right nut to run my tongue along the side of her perfect, untouched neck. To taste the saltiness of her unease as it prickles along her flesh like a delicious little snack for a monster like me. I would nibble at her tiny earlobe with the tiny diamond stud and whisper hot, dirty things into her ear.

Crossing my arms over my chest, I glance over at the clock. Ten minutes. I have ten minutes until I need to get out into the main part of the club to listen to Soul Prison. She has ten minutes to come over here and do whatever damage she plans on doing.

And she better cut deep, hard, and fast.

Because if she doesn't...I'll be coming for her.

There's no way I can't pursue the fuck out of this woman now. Not when I've fantasized about making her face turn purple and her throat bruised by my fingers. She should have stayed the fuck away. I would've left her alone. Tried to forget about how fucking enticing she was in the courtroom.

But now?

Little lamb, you've fucked up by coming to the lion's den.

I'm hungry for you, baby.

I have your scent now.

There's no getting away.

TWO

NATASHA

He's disgusting. I hate him.

How can that woman do that to him in full view of everyone?

Gross. And weird, too.

Her head bobs up and down like she's going for gold and yet he's not even paying attention to her ministrations. Warm, acquisitive eyes scan the room until they find me and stop.

A twist of his lips sends a flood of heat to my cheeks and between my thighs.

Ugh, focus, Natasha.

Some of these places he likes to come to are just a cesspit for drunks and whores, both men and women. The air stinks of cheap perfume, lousy beer, sweat, and bodily fluids. I'm going to need to get checked at the clinic after just coming in here.

I sense other men's eyes on me, but the only ones having any effect are *his*.

The bastard.

I detest him and his influence on my body more than anything in this world. My body doesn't contain the same rage my mind does. I hate how I can know what he is—a monster, a pervert, a murdering creep —yet my body still reacts like every other damn woman who's around him. *Lust*. Primal and achingly present whenever I see him.

Pleasure washes over his face, the muscles in his body tensing as the blonde on her knees gags on his release. Disgusting. *Beautiful*. When she pulls away, I catch a glint of silver on the tip of his dick. A piercing. I'm ridiculously curious, but refuse to entertain that thought for even one second longer.

He fastens his jeans, his eyes never leaving my direction. *Good*. I want him to see me. To know I'm watching.

I'll haunt him for *her*. I won't let him forget her and what he did.

Sending the woman on her way forces a snort from me. The disappointment on her face is comical. She looks older than him by at least a decade, and yet has the same pining in her eyes as most of the college age girls here, hoping at a shot with the bad boy Ren Hayes. His reputation is more famous than half the bands he's helped launch.

The swagger he has screams confidence—in charge—not a care in the world. But he's a murderer.

Convincing the strangers on the jury—who didn't even know Kate—that he didn't kill her, may have come naturally to him, but he didn't trick me with his lies. I know what he did, and so does *he.*

He didn't just kill my best friend, he stole a part of me in the process.

Kate and I weren't just friends. We grew up together, shared dreams, went to school together, lived together.

We were best friends, and he snuffed out her light. The asshole got away with it, making her out to be some fetish queen. Kate was as straitlaced as they come. I would have known if she was into kinky sex. She would have told me. *Wouldn't she?*

Ignoring the faint whisperings of my subconscious, I narrow my eyes at Ren. As much as I remind myself he's a killer, it doesn't stop me from coming here, from seeking him out.

I'm not afraid of him. Not in the way I should be. But I can't figure out why the hell not.

My chest constricts when he begins walking my way. I hate the conflicting ramblings of my mind that send a flutter of attraction below my waist as my eyes track over his well-formed body.

Worn leather boots track a path to me. Jeans caressing his legs and hanging low on his hips scream rock star. A band tee and a leather jacket cover his torso. A chiseled jaw, thick lips, and straight nose accompany deep oval-shaped eyes the color of rich, dark chocolate to complete his beautiful face. His hair is a dark, messy mop that sits in disarray over his head.

That stupid face had every female juror melting in their seats and every male wishing they were him.

There's a charm about him that's intoxicating if you allow yourself to be bewitched by it.

Anxiety niggles away at me, making me fidget and play with my glasses. I refuse to squirm under the scrutiny of his gaze. I won't allow him to see how out of my comfort zone I am.

I've learned everything I can about who he is. I know all the bars he visits—where he lives—where he works. The Internet is a powerful tool, free to us all. No one can be anonymous in this day and age.

Folding my arms over my chest, I glare up at him as his boots stop almost on top of my tennis shoes.

So close.

I can almost taste the sweat beading on the flesh of his neck.

"You've been eye-fucking me, sweetheart. You want to play out those fantasizes flashing through that innocent, little head of yours or just observe while someone else does?"

"You're an animal," I snap, disgust rippling through me.

The curl of his lip makes my stomach dip.

"That's what intrigues you, though, isn't it, Natasha?" He caresses my name over his tongue, making every letter sound dirty.

Many times, our eyes clashed during his trial. A thousand words were shared without making a sound. He knows who I am, just like I know who he is. We're connected in the most fucked up of ways.

Music thuds to the sound of my heartbeat as the atmosphere thickens and pulses around us.

Looking down at the watch on his wrist, he mutters under his breath, and then taps his finger on the watch face. "I only have five minutes, gorgeous.

Still, I'm sure I can make you come in that time. Although," he purrs, closing in around me, robbing me of breath, "I'm pretty certain you're halfway there already. Like to watch, do you?"

Slamming my hands on his firm chest, I attempt to force him away, but his body doesn't even flinch at my attack. Hard muscles tense against the skin of my palms.

Damn, he's like granite to touch. I want to explore the rest of him.

No, you don't.

Chuckling, he looks down at my fingers splayed across him. A wicked spark flashes in his brown eyes, sending a quivering ache through my body. I sag in response, hating myself for having any reaction to his good looks. My hands drop to my sides like the mere touch of him burns. A stinging sensation forms in my eyes, threatening to show my vulnerability and weakness.

Please don't cry.

Please don't cry.

I hate myself. I hate him. *You want him.*

Tracing his eyes over my face, his brow drops and then he's moving back a step. A cool whoosh of air saturates me, making me sigh in relief. I need the reprieve from having his dominating presence so close. He overwhelms me, his proximity a storm of chaotic emotions swirling my insides, leaving me a muddled and confused puddle.

"Time's up," he says with a wicked wink. "See you around, Nat."

Bastard.

"Yes, you will," I spit out. "You'll be seeing me everywhere." I square my shoulders, taking a step toward him, filling with a bravado that's usually foreign to me. "I'm going to be everywhere you turn. You will see so much of me. I'll be there when you close your eyes at night. I'll remind you every day of what you are, what you did, all this," I snap, gesturing to him from head to toe. "You may convince everyone else that you're too pretty to be a killer, but not me. You're a murderer, Ren Hayes. I won't let you forget that."

All air rushes from my lungs when he closes back in on me lightning quick. Chills scatter over my flesh, causing the skin to rise with goose bumps. A pit of dread forms in my stomach. My back hits the wall behind me as his hand comes up to my neck, but doesn't close around me. Instead, he hovers his palm there.

A threat of what he could do. What he wants to do. The action an echo of how Kate died.

"I hope you're prepared to be pushed far out of your comfort zone then, precious. Because forcing yourself into my world is a daring thing to do." His breath whispers over my ear, brushing my hair with his lips. My chest heaves with ragged breaths as I attempt to drag air into my lungs. "The Ren Hayes you're speaking of sounds like a dangerous man," he finishes as he pulls away slightly, his eyes stroking over every inch of my face, ending at my lips.

"Maybe I'm a dangerous woman," I choke out.

Grinning, he pushes away from me. "We'll see about that."

And then he's gone, disappearing from the VIP room and back into the club, leaving me a gasping mess.

THREE

REN

A week later…

Sweat coats my skin, dripping down my torso. Every part of me is on fire. I take the girl from behind, her blond hair gripped in my fist as I force my cock all the way to the hilt inside her. Moans hum through the room in sync with my punishing thrusts.

“Choke me, fucking choke me,” the bitch begs.

“Shut up,” I growl. The rule I gave her was she doesn’t get to fucking speak.

I have someone else in my mind, and this bitch's voice is ruining the fantasy.

My hand slips over her shoulder and up to her neck. Her pulse jumps under my palm. I tighten my fist, cutting off her airway.

Juices spurt over my cock from the mere touch of my skin on her neck.

Tugging her head back further and giving her throat a little squeeze has her coming completely undone. Spasms rack over her body, her orgasm violent and unsatisfying for me.

Pulling out of her, I release her hair and neck before yanking off my condom. I stroke my cock, my thumb rubbing over the silver ball of my piercing, with another blonde in mind until my load empties over her ass.

"I've been waiting nearly a year to get in this room with you," she pants, collapsing on the bed.

It fucking shows. She was ready to combust before we even got naked. I have a reputation at this club. Hush is my favorite and members only. It's for all kinds of kinks and fetishes. I'm good friends with the owner, Joshua Tuck. We've known each other since before he opened this place, and I've been around to watch it become one of the most desirable clubs to have a membership with. There are a couple of Doms, along with myself, who have a wait list here at Hush. When the women are like Amber, however, it makes the whole scene feel tacky and forced.

Walking over to the adjacent bathroom, I wash my hands and splash cold water over my face. A shower would feel better, but this will do for now. Amber chatters on about next time—*there won't be a next time*—while I brood over a certain blonde who has me all tied up in knots.

A rap on the door saves me from having to spend any more time than necessary in here with this joke of a woman and I flee the bathroom, eager for the interruption. She doesn't have a fetish. She just likes good-looking cock, rougher than she'd get it at home from her husband. Amber wouldn't know real breathplay even if I throttled her into unconsciousness.

Slipping my jeans up my thighs, I saunter to the door and unlock it. Axel, the head of security, stands before me—all six feet seven of him.

"Sorry to interrupt, Ren, but there's a woman out front asking everyone questions about you. Do you want her gone?"

Motherfucker.

How the fuck did she get in here? The little troublemaker has been everywhere lately, at every fucking turn, but here? I thought this would be the one place she wouldn't come into.

Storming down the corridor, I barge onto the club floor and scan the room.

I spot her from a mile away. She stands out like a grandma at a frat party.

Her innocent look and inexperienced aura is like a fucking neon sign making every dick in this place rock fucking hard. All attention falls on me as I storm over to her, wearing nothing but my unbuckled jeans.

Her back is to me as she talks animatedly to two Doms, who are lapping up her naivety.

She must sense me coming because her body visibly tenses. Her shoulders straighten as she slowly turns to face me. The two guys she was talking to watch me over her shoulder, eyes heavy with intrigue and lust evident in their expressions.

"Ren, speak of the devil." One of them named Nick sluggishly grins.

"How the fuck did you get in here?" I growl down at her, ignoring them.

"I paid for my membership like everyone else." She smirks with a shrug of her shoulders, proud of herself.

Reaching out, I grasp her wrist, causing a startled

gasp to leave her plush, full lips. The tantalizing sound of it makes my dick jump.

"Let go of me, you murderer," she snarls, trying to free herself.

I'm sick to death of hearing that fucking word aimed at me.

A raised eyebrow from both guys makes me fucking fume. "Mind your damn business," I growl at them and drag her across the room.

She struggles when I push through the doors to the corridor leading back to the room I just left. Shoving her inside the room, she squeals and then screws her face up when she sees Amber still inside getting dressed.

"Out," I bark, making Amber's mouth pop open. She looks between us both and licks her lips.

"I can stay," Amber offers, smiling as she cuts her greedy eyes over to Natasha.

"Gross," Nat snaps, shuddering.

Amber narrows her eyes and folds her arms over her bought chest. "Rude, little bitch."

Snatching up her shirt, Amber sashays over to me and pulls it over her head. When she reaches me, she grabs my face in her palms, forcing me down to her mouth. Her lips smack loudly with mine as she makes a show of it, and I let her. Teeth nip and her tongue tastes me. Then, she's smirking over at Nat before leaving the room with a wave of her fingers.

Natasha wrinkles her nose as she walks over to the disheveled bed. "So, you have sex with people in here?"

"Why? You want to go for a ride?" I tease.

"Over my dead body," she stutters on the last word, and her brow crashes over her pretty green eyes.

Her best friend's death is haunting her.

"Calm down, Nat. If I wanted to kill you, I wouldn't bring you in here to do it." I flick my eyes up to the camera in the corner of the room and wink over at her.

"Oh, I know how and where you like to kill people." She means the cheap apartment building over on Beller Square. Strangled to death. Just like Kate was found. Anger replaces her sorrow from moments before. "They film you having sex in here? With women like that?" She scowls, pointing to the door, clearly referring to Amber.

"The camera is for safety reasons. To protect the club if an accident should happen or if anyone breaks the rules, and what's wrong with Amber?" I ask just to fuck with her.

"She's tacky for one and more plastic than flesh

for another. And rules, really, Ren? Where were your rules when you killed Kate?" she sneers, her mouth cruel and biting, but her eyes drink in my bare chest hungrily, betraying her.

Anger is a powerful tool, but also a damaging one. It can eat you up and leave nothing but a bitter taste in your mouth.

"Kate was into this scene, no matter how much you want to think otherwise," I tell her.

Her feet rush over to me, and a tiny palm slaps across my cheek, sending a spark of fire across my skin and into my dick. *She's fucking cute.*

"You don't get to speak her name. Your lies won't work on me. I knew her. I know she wouldn't be into this disgusting shit. Fucking in clubs on camera for God knows who to see?"

"Don't knock it until you've tried it," I growl, loving the curse words on her sweet lips.

"Tell me. Tell me how you did it." She chokes on her words. "Was she in pain? Did she know she was going to die?"

Sighing, I run my hands through my hair and pace the floor.

"Why are you so damn sure it was murder? There were no signs of struggle, no defensive wounds. She was in the height of pleasure. An accident that should never have happened."

Tears drip from her eyes, making them appear impossibly bright.

"Why wouldn't I know that she was into that? What could she get out of being strangled?" she weeps.

"It's breathplay, Nat. It's not safe and shouldn't be practiced by most people who do it. But they do it all the same. For the thrill."

"Including you," she spits out, wiping at the tears on her cheeks. "You still killed her."

"I've never killed anyone."

"Liar." She seethes, her fists clenching.

"Believe what you want, and keep following me around all you want too, but it's not going to bring her back or change the facts."

"And what are the facts?" she demands, her voice shrill. "I need them to be able to move on. I need to know everything. Just give me that."

Stalking across the room to her, I cause her feet to falter. Her legs hit the bed, making her lose her balance. She topples backward, her ass hitting the mattress.

"How much is everything, Nat?" I breathe, pulling my belt from my jeans with a snap. I place it over her shoulder and across her neck. I don't add any pressure, but her expressive eyes expand nonetheless. Her hands go to the leather, immediately threading her fingers behind it to protect herself from me tightening if I wanted to. And I do want to more than anything, but I'm not the monster she thinks I am.

"I hate you," she sobs, yanking the belt from her neck and pushing up from the bed before heading for the door.

Fuck if I'm allowing her to run away with that lie on her lips.

Trailing her, I grasp her shoulder, spinning her and backing her against the wall. I'm quick with my skilled fingers, flicking through the buttons of her jeans. I open and shove my hand down into her panties before she can process what I'm doing.

Her hand grips my wrist as a rush of air exhales from her lips. "Ren," she gasps out, breathless and achingly desperate.

"Hate me, huh?" I smile, smug as shit. Her juices spread over my fingers. She's fucking soaked, her pussy swollen and begging for attention. She doesn't hate me.

"I do," she pants as I slip a finger inside her tight cunt.

Her pupils dilate, her grip tightening on my wrist. She raises onto her tiptoes, pushing down on my arm, trying to force me out of her, but her fight isn't as convincing as she wants it to be because not once has she tried to move away. Not once has she said no. Stop.

Fight me.

Tell me no, little lamb.

You want this.

I want this.

"You may hate me, Nat, but your body doesn't. Quite the fucking opposite. Do you want me to take away your ache?" I whisper against her cheek. Her face turns away from me. "Look at me."

"I can't," she sobs, dropping her feet down and allowing my finger to slide deeper inside her.

A delicious little mewl sounds from her lips, making my cock strain with need.

"I hate you." Tears roll down her cheeks, but she rocks her hips forward. It's subtle, but I feel her movements and sigh against her. She wants this, *me.*

I'll bleed this fury from her quivering body, but not now. Not like this in a room soaked with the scent of sex from me and Amber.

Pulling my finger from inside her and my hand from her panties, I wipe my fingers over her lips, letting her taste her own need for me. "Keep telling yourself that you hate me. I guess I'm not the only liar in the room, Nat."

Sniffling, she turns for the door and runs from the room.

My cock screams for me to chase her down. Devour the lamb like the wolf I am. But I don't. Instead, I bring my fingers to my nose and inhale her sweet fucking scent before sucking them into my mouth and then stroking the ache from my cock to the taste of her on my tongue.

FOUR

NATASHA

I pace around my studio apartment, attempting to talk myself off the proverbial ledge. What the hell was I thinking last night? All day I couldn't focus on my classes. One of my professors even yelled at me. Me! I'm usually a teacher's favorite. Certainly don't get yelled at for daydreaming. I call it night-maring while awake.

Over and over again, images of the way his hand dove into my pants and touched me played in my mind. I hated it. I hate him.

Oh my God, I'm such a liar.

Which makes me a sick girl.

Truth is, I loved it. On some deep level, I was completely turned on. By a murderer. I wait for the normal venom and hate to be stabbed mentally at Ren, but tonight, I come up empty.

I didn't kill her.

The same words he spoke to the jury, but this time, I actually felt doubt in my accusations. If he didn't kill her, who did? Until last night, I hadn't really considered another suspect. It was Ren. His smug grin and hot face weren't fooling me.

But maybe my ability to read people sucks.

I thought I knew Kate. She was my best friend. We did everything together. *Not everything.* We told each other everything. *Not everything.*

So Kate was into kinky stuff and was too shy to tell me?

Or afraid I'd judge her.

Shame burns through me. I've been known to bark out my distaste over certain things while watching shows. I didn't know it impacted her, though. Kept her from telling me her deepest, darkest secrets.

I'm sorry, Kate.

Had I known, maybe I could have gone with you. I could have protected you.

I think back to the week before she died. She'd vaguely mentioned seeing someone. Never mentioned his name, but told me he wore expensive suits and was going to be famous one day.

Ren doesn't wear suits.

I rush into my bedroom and pull out her box of belongings I was allowed to keep that her parents didn't want. Our old apartment was gorgeous and overlooked the good parts of the city. My new apartment is lonely and faces a brick wall. I'd live in an apartment in the ghetto as long as I had her back and lived with her. God, I miss her.

The box is mostly filled with pictures of us, a bunch of notebooks she was always doodling in, and other miscellaneous stuff that I picked up from our place that reminded me of her. I flip through the notebooks, searching for more clues.

I come across a note scribbled between big drawings of roses that makes the hairs on my arms stand on end.

He doesn't love her. She's an accessory to him. I'm real. I know he won't marry her. Not when he has me on the side. I know what he likes because I like it too. It has to be enough.

I need to talk to Ren.

My flesh heats as I think about the last time we "talked." It ended with his hand down my pants. And before I let him strip me and fuck me on the bed he'd just used with some sick whore, he sent me on my way. That hurt, but in a way, I was more than relieved. Not because I didn't want to sleep with Ren —because in that moment, I so did—but because I didn't want to be leftovers.

Stupid girl.

Stupid, stupid girl.

I'm not going to sleep with him. I'm just going to talk with him.

Ripping the note from the notebook, I fold it and shove it into my jeans pocket. I make a pass through the bathroom to make sure I look okay. My blond waves are messy and I have dark circles under my eyes from lack of sleep. I look like shit. Good, maybe he'll stay back and let me talk.

I pull my phone out from my back pocket and check Twitter. Ren is a social media nut. He doesn't miss a beat on letting the whole damn world know his location. It's why I find him so easily. It's like he wants to be found.

Tonight he's listening to a band called Berlin Scandal at a dive bar called Stuckey's. He's tweeted seven times commenting on their unique alternative sound and how radio stations should be playing their songs because "these guys are gonna blow up." People eat up the hype and he already has thousands of retweets. I feel crappy about crashing in on a work thing, but this can't wait. I need to talk to him.

I take a cab downtown and fly out of the vehicle after tossing some bills at the driver. The cover is twenty freaking dollars, but the line to get in is wrapped around the entire building. No doubt thanks to Ren's tweets.

I'm about to give in and just opt to wait until later when the bar empties. That is, until the door guy crooks a finger at me to come to the front of the line. Biting my lip, I go to him, ignoring the huffs and curses from the people behind me.

"Lose the jacket," he demands.

Rolling my eyes, I slip the jean jacket off, tie it around my waist, and then look up at him expectantly, knowing full well my shirt is skintight and more revealing than anything I'd usually wear. It was one of Kate's that she bought but didn't fit into.

Grinning down at my cleavage, he places a lanyard over my head that says *groupie* splashed across it.

Gross.

He then opens the door and slaps my ass, shooing me inside.

As soon as I burst into the dark bar, heavy guitar riffs assault me. The bass thumps and the drummer is pounding away. I hate to admit it, but Ren's right. These guys are good. Pushing through the crowd, I make my way toward the front. I'm short and skinny, so I slide in between people easily. When I make it up to the front and grip the fencing keeping the people back, I turn my head left and right, seeking Ren out.

Nowhere.

Where the hell is he?

Someone presses into me from behind. Some asshole who reeks of hard liquor. When I push back, he nuzzles my hair.

"Come home with me," the drunk bellows, his hand roaming up my bare arm.

I freeze, panicked at his boldness. I push against him again, but he's stronger than me. His erection pokes my back. Before I can freak out, he's jerked away from me. Powerful hands grip my hips and spin me around. As soon as my eyes meet familiar brown ones, I sag in relief.

His mouth moves, but I can't hear what he's saying. Concern flashes in his eyes, confusing me.

When he grips my throat in a gentle, but possessive way, I don't freak out. He leans forward, bringing his mouth to my ear.

"Are you okay?" he yells above the music.

I nod, blinking away the tears. Since when did the enemy become my savior? His thumb caresses the flesh on my throat, lingering on where my blood pumps rapidly through my jugular vein.

"If you're going to stalk me, at least ride with me to these places," he barks at me. "This shithole is only good for one thing. The music. You have to watch these assholes, though. They're grabby and mouthy and always looking for a fight. You're not safe here alone."

The crowd pushes him from behind, making his hard body press against mine. I grip the sides of his T-shirt to keep from falling to the floor. One of his hands circles around me, resting on the small of my back. He pulls me into him. My heart rate races when I realize it's not because he's copping a feel, but because he's protecting me from being smashed into the fence. His breath is hot on my ear, but he doesn't talk again, he nips at my earlobe.

Heat, explosive and fiery, burns all the way to my core. Instead of pushing him away, I angle my head to the side, giving him the access he needs. His grip on my neck tightens and I can feel how aroused he is since he's pressed against me.

"Look how brave you are," he rumbles into my ear. "I have you in my grip, little lamb. I'm going to bite you and steal your breath. Why aren't you running?"

My heart stammers in my chest. His words should be frightening, but I'm turned on instead. I need to talk to him. But right now, in this moment, I want him to do exactly what he threatens.

Why?

Why do I want this?

Because you want him, crazy girl.

His grip on my throat tightens, constricting my airway. Just hard enough that I can still suck in air, but it comes at the cost of making my face burn with the effort. The music is too loud to hear the rasping of my labored breathing, but the air claws its way into my lungs.

"So brave and curious," he growls. "Coming, while struggling for air, is unlike any orgasm you've ever had before. I'm going to hold you down, make you fight for air, and pleasure you until you climax so hard you black out." He bites my neck below my earlobe as promised. The sting feels good. "And then I'll rouse you with kisses to your perfect tits. Kiss my way down to your sweet cunt that drips just for me. You wanted to know why she liked it, how it felt. I'll show you."

"I don't want to die."

"You won't," he promises with a labored groan. "You will come alive."

I let out an embarrassing moan. Thank God no one can hear.

His palm slides up to my jaw, allowing me to breathe freely. Fingers bite into my skin and he tilts my face to meet his. Intense, brown eyes burn into me. I can't hear his words, but I can see them.

I'm. Going. To. Kiss. You. Now.

My eyes flutter closed when his mouth nears mine. His lips are soft as they brush against mine. I part my lips, allowing him the access he clearly wants—what we both clearly want. He darts his tongue out and it easily dominates mine.

Oh God.

I'm kissing Ren Hayes.

What's wrong with me?

Right now, it feels so right.

He tastes like mint gum and I am relieved that he doesn't seem to have been drinking. My tongue lashes with his as I taste him to be sure. Nope. No beer. Just yummy mint. His palm at my back slides under my tank top. Fingers on my back have me shivering. My nipples harden and my pussy aches.

Ren is so smooth.

Too smooth.

The thought of all the other women he goes to bed with has me stiffening. He breaks our kiss to frown at me. As much as I want to kiss him longer, I can't. I came to see him for a reason.

"We need to talk," I yell over the music.

"I can't hear you," he bellows back, smirking.

Damn him and his devilishly handsome good looks.

Feeling bold, I slide my hands up his chest to his neck, pulling him closer. My lips brush against his ear. "We need to talk."

I refrain from biting his ear since he bit mine, and instead lean back to look at him. His lips crash to mine and he kisses me deeply once more until I'm dizzy. I manage to pull away, giving him a stern look that has him laughing.

A thrill runs up my spine when he finds my ear again. "I heard you the first time. I just wanted to kiss your pretty mouth again."

Ugh. He's such an arrogant shit.

He winks at me before grabbing my hand to guide me away from the drunk assholes. As we make our way through the crowd, I groan at my inability to tell him no. Was this how it was for Kate? Did she just follow the wolf right into his den?

His hand squeezes mine and he looks over his shoulder, the concerned look back in his expressive brown eyes.

I'm having trouble matching up Ren to the monster I once thought he was.

He may not have killed Kate, but he's not telling me everything. I need to know the truth. Everything he knew about Kate and the "suit" she was so clearly obsessed with.

I'll get the truth out of him one way or another.

FIVE

REN

One taste. One taste and I'm fucking addicted. Just like I knew I would be. I want to ask her where her sexy glasses are. Why she's wearing a top that's more a second skin than clothing. And who the fuck stuck a groupie lanyard on her. But words get lost on my lips when her eyes storm with questions. Nerdy Natasha didn't come all the way to the shitty part of town to make out with my sexy ass. No, she came here probably to accuse me some more.

Accusers don't usually let you stick your tongue down their throat, though.

Tonight, she's let me kiss her, bite her, and fucking squeeze her pretty throat. All it did was awaken the beast inside of me. My beast is hungry for her. It won't be sated until it's feasted on her. I drag her outside and pull my phone out. Quickly, I text Ronan. Berlin Scandal is badass. We're signing them. Tomorrow I'll call them and give them the good news. Earlier, before the show, they seemed so hopeful. Most bands want to be signed by Harose. These kids are lucky because their dream is about to come true.

I find my midnight blue 2020 Porsche 911 and hit the key fob to unlock it. Natasha gives me a wary look as she tugs on her jean jacket, but when I open the passenger side door, she slides into the car. I close the door and then join her inside. The engine purrs like a kitten. Zipping out onto the road, I throw her an expectant look.

"You wanted to talk?" I ask, weaving in between cars.

"Where are we going?" she squeaks out in return.

Not this again. "Jesus, Nat. I'm not going to kill you. It's getting old."

"I don't think you're going to kill me," she huffs. "I just want to know where we're going. Are you always a dick?"

Smirking at her, I shrug. "Honestly, the only person I'm a dick to is you. You bring out that endearing quality."

"Asshole," she mumbles.

"You hungry?"

"Yeah."

Her response shocks me, but I don't let it show. Instead, I whip through a drive thru. We order a couple of value meals and then I head back home. She munches on fries almost happily. Noted. *I'll feed your pretty mouth if that improves your mood, beautiful.*

I pass my brother's gated community and drive to my condo. He'd lectured my ass for weeks when I didn't buy a house, but instead bought a condominium. I'm one guy who's hardly ever home. I don't need a giant, empty house like Ronan. It's depressing as fuck.

As soon as we pull into the underground garage and park, I grab our food and my drink, leaving her with just her drink. We take the elevator until we're on the top floor. I unlock the door and push inside my condo that smells like cinnamon. It's something that only my brother knows. Cinnamon reminds me of Mom—of home—so it's the one thing I always have. The cinnamon scented candles are the same kind she used before cancer took her twelve years ago when I was a junior in high school.

I drop our food on the coffee table, kick off my boots, and then drop onto the middle cushion of the sofa. Natasha remains rooted by the door, but eventually she mimics my action. Her tennis shoes get left beside my boots and she sits next to me. We eat in comfortable silence. It isn't until we've tossed the wrappers into the bag that she speaks again.

"I found a note. I think it means something," she says, turning her troubled face my way. Her green eyes flicker with uncertainty as she digs in her pocket. Once she pulls out the note and hands it to me, I tense.

He doesn't love her. She's an accessory to him. I'm real. I know he won't marry her. Not when he has me on the side. I know what he likes because I like it too. It has to be enough.

"You never had a fiancée."

Fuck.

She really is a little detective.

"You got me," I deadpan.

She rolls her eyes. "You also don't wear suits."

"Fuck no," I bark out. "That's more my brother's gig."

Her brows furl together. "Is your brother engaged?"

Oh, hell no.

"Ronan didn't kill Kate," I bark out, my urge to protect my brother rising up inside me like the swell of a tide.

She studies me for a moment. "I believe you."

A laugh bursts from me. "Since when?"

"You just have to push," she snaps. "I'm *trying* to be nice."

"If you have to try, it's not genuine," I tease.

"You didn't kill my best friend. But I think you know who did."

"You should take off your pants," I suggest, changing the subject.

She parts her lips, shocked at my words, so I kiss that surprised mouth of hers. Her tongue tastes salty from her fries. I devour her perfect mouth as my hands greedily tug at her jean jacket.

"Ren," she groans, breaking our kiss. "What are you doing?"

"Getting you naked," I rumble.

"I think we shouldn't..."

"Shhh, sweetness, you think way too much. Just feel for once."

I pull her jean jacket off and then her tank top, making her shiver. Her black bra lifts her full tits in the most deliciously tempting way. I need to see her nipples. Pushing her back against the cushions, I tug down at the cups on her bra, freeing each breast. Her rosy pink nipples are hard. Each one begs to be bitten and licked. Her gulp is audible, making me hungry. I waste no time putting one in my mouth. I suck hard enough to make her cry out, then soothe away the hurt with my tongue. Her breaths come out ragged and desperate. I make quick work of undoing her jeans. A nervous whine escapes her when I jerk them down her thighs along with her panties. Her smooth cunt is tempting as fuck. I cannot wait to suck every bit of her essence from those pale lips between her thighs.

"Ren," she whimpers. "Oh, God, what am I doing? I came here to talk."

I kiss down her stomach, darting my eyes up to hers. "If you wanted to talk, you would have talked to me outside of that bar. When you got inside my car, you wanted to fuck. And, sweetheart, I'm here to please."

Gripping her thighs, I pull her apart, opening her pink cunt to me. Her opening is slick with arousal that makes my dick harder than ever. I dip down and run my tongue up her slit, tasting her sweetness.

"Ohhhhh," she whines.

I circle her clit with my tongue. This makes her jerk with pleasure. *That's it, baby, let me make you feel good. You won't want to talk because you'll be too busy screaming.*

A woman like Natasha is easy to please. She's always so tense and wrapped up in her head, that if you pleasure her even for a few minutes, she lets go of all that baggage and takes a sin trip with me. Like now, her back arches up off the sofa and she moans loudly. Her cunt drips with her need. I greedily lap it up, devouring her sweet taste. The moment I tug at her throbbing clit with my teeth, she detonates like a fucking bomb. Her scream is loud enough to wake the dead. As she comes down from her high, I lick her clit once more before yanking off my T-shirt. Her eyes are fluttered closed and her chest heaves with exertion. While she's distracted, I find a condom from my wallet, push my jeans and boxers down, and roll on the rubber.

Her thighs start to close, but I settle my big body between them, loving the flare of lust in her green eyes. Gripping my dick, I tease her slick opening, my eyebrow lifted in question.

Holding on by a thread here, baby.

She plants her heels into my ass, giving me all the permission I need. Without any warning, I drive all the way into her tight heat.

"Oh my God," she whines. "I can feel it. It feels so—ahh!"

I thrust hard, letting my piercing do its job. "I know, baby. So fucking good. Feels amazing for me too."

Her eyes flutter closed again as she tosses her head back, baring her perfect neck to me. As I punish her cunt with my aching cock, I seek out her neck. At first I suckle the flesh and nip at it. But it's not enough. Softly gripping her throat, I lift up slightly so I can see her face. Her lips part as panicked green eyes meet mine. Her cunt clenches, though. She loves the thrill just like I knew she would.

"Making good on my promise from earlier," I tell her with a crooked grin. I bite her bottom lip, loving the way she squeezes around my dick once more. "You're going to love this, Nat. I'll take it slow. Count with me in your mind. Three seconds," I tell her as I move my palm up to just under her jaw line. I tighten my hand on her neck, not enough to cut off her oxygen, just restrict the amount she can take in. I suck on her bottom lip, all the while thrusting into her.

One.

Thrust.

Two.

Thrust.

Three.

Thrust.

Release.

She gasps and grinds her hips against me. "Again," she pleads.

"Five this time," I warn her.

One.

Thrust.

Two.

Thrust.

Three.

Thrust.

Four.

Thrust.

Five.

Thrust.

Release.

She gasps, sucking at the air to fill her burning

lungs. Pupils shot, body deliriously flying on the high. My mark bruising her flesh sends ripples of heat through my body. Fuck. She's so much more than a little lamb. She's a wolf willing to submit to her Alpha.

"Again," she breathes.

The tighter I squeeze, the more purple her face turns. *One.* The fatter her bottom lip seems to get. *Two.* Her fingernails dig into my biceps, gouging me, and it only serves to turn me on more. *Three.* I tighten my grip, nearly constricting her airflow altogether. Her breath—what little of it that can travel through—rasps through her nearly closed airway.

"You're so fucking beautiful," I praise, kissing her plump lips, stealing more of her breath. "So perfect." *Four.*

I pull away from her mouth, pinning her by her throat against the sofa. Using my other hand, I rub at her clit. Her body jolts and spasms beneath me. Her hands grip my arm as though she might want to claw at me and pull me away, but based on the way her hips meet mine thrust for thrust, she's so fucking needy for this kinky thrill only I can offer her. *Five.*

"More," she begs, unrestrained. Her body is painted in red bruises. Sweat sprinkling over every inch of her flesh nearly has me losing my control.

"More." She grinds against me, desperate and wild. Once again, I tighten my hold.

"Seven, beautiful," I croon. "Let's go until you're on the edge of bliss and push you over."

Strumming her clit while seizing her breath drives her fucking crazy. Look how perfect she is. *One.* Her body was created to be dominated—to be breathless—free on the edge of euphoria and beyond it. *Two.* She was always meant for this—for pleasure—for me. *Three.*

A few more strokes has her entire body seizing in pleasure. *Four.* Knowing she'll want air, I grip her throat tight enough that nothing will go in or out. *Five.* She's so lost in the pleasure that she chooses an orgasm over air. *Six.* And the orgasm she chose doesn't disappoint her. It goes on and on and on. *Seven.* When she seems seconds from passing out, I release her neck and come down to kiss her again. She's unmoving but still conscious as I kiss her. Her tongue swipes along mine, showing she's still here with me and enjoying this, which causes my nuts to tighten. I come with a pleased groan, flexing my ass muscles as I grind as deep into her tight body as I can get.

Resting against her slick body, I nuzzle my nose to her ear. "Now that was amazing."

Her fingernails run down my ribs and I shiver. The touch is so intimate that I almost shy away from it. I should have known Natasha would be different from everyone else. Because right now, I want to carry her off to my bed and sleep with her. Like turn the lights off and fucking cuddle.

I'm Ren fucking Hayes.

I don't cuddle.

I choke and suck and fuck.

But one yawn from Nat and it's clear to me.

Tonight, I'm going to cuddle, goddammit.

SIX

NATASHA

I wake shrouded in darkness. A warm arm draped over my naked body keeps me pinned to the soft mattress I'm lying on. It offers comfort in an odd way, for reasons I don't want to dissect right now. I vaguely remember moving to Ren's bedroom at some point in the night, but wasn't planning on staying over. My hand snakes up to touch my bruised neck. I never dreamed I'd enjoy such violent beauty in the bedroom. Not that I'm all that experienced in the bedroom department. I've had a couple of boyfriends, and the only boundaries they pushed was a finger in the butt.

Ren brought more orgasms out of my body in this one night than my previous boyfriends have in our entire relationships combined.

And his piercing?

My mind is blown. Who knew a thick rod of metal with balls on each end could hit unimaginable places within you? When I asked to take a closer peek at it, he was all too accommodating. It ended with his dick in my mouth, and honestly, I was thrilled to give back a little torturous pleasure. Knowing I can make him groan and curse with just my tongue is empowering.

Peeling Ren's arm from me, I slip out of the bed and tiptoe out of the bedroom and into the living room. Searching the space, I quietly gather up my discarded clothes. My cheeks heat when I scoop up my panties from the bottom of the couch. An echo of sensation hums through my body as memories flood my mind.

Damn you, Ren Hayes.

Skimming my panties up my legs, I startle when a deep groan sounds from the doorway. I must have woken him because Ren stands there watching me.

His silhouette is outlined in the hue of the moonlight creeping in through the window bare of curtains.

"You're quite the sight bent over like that, Nat," he croons.

Warmth floods my pussy, the crimson glow still burning in my cheeks igniting further.

"What are you doing?" he asks, devouring me with just his eyes.

"Getting dressed," I answer, slipping my panties into place. My tone is laced in arousal, even to my own ears. What's he doing to me? *Awakening you.*

"Why?" He leans against the frame completely naked. His eyes are surveying every inch of me on display for him. Just like I drink in every solid plane of his physique on display for me. Finishing at his hard cock saluting me from across the room.

Saliva floods my mouth, and I have to swallow to be able to speak. "I should go," I say, but it has no conviction.

"Why?" He smirks, prowling toward me, making my breath hitch. "I'm not done with you yet," he adds with a dark tone.

All thoughts of leaving vanish.

He moves so fast I don't have time to flee his advance. Not that I want to. His shoulder connects with my midriff as he leans down to toss me over his shoulder and marches us back to his bedroom.

I land on the bed with a gentle thud, the air whooshing around me making my nipples peak. His soft footfalls sound through the room and then light floods the space.

"I want to see every part of you," he announces as I track his movements around the bed. I didn't see anything when he brought me in here earlier tonight because it was pitch-black, but now I see everything in the glow of the unforgiving light. *There's no hiding from him.*

His bed is a four-poster with dark silk drapes connecting each pillar. Picking up some of the material, he drapes it over my ankle and then ties it before moving to my other foot.

"What are you doing?" I ask, not sure if I want to aid him or flee. I'm in too deep. *Not deep enough.*

"Playing." He grins wickedly.

Tugging the fabric tight around my flesh, he admires my spread legs and crawls between them. I lean forward to meet him, but his hands grasp my wrists and he forces me down flat against the mattress, his weight hovering above me.

"Do you trust me?" he whispers against my lips, making me quiver with need. His hard cock grinds against my panty-covered pussy. I regret putting them back on instantly and unabashedly rise up to meet his pressure.

"Do you trust me?" he repeats, groaning from our contact.

"No," I tell him. But I'm unsure if it's truth or a lie.

Dragging his lips across my jaw, he bites down, making me arch into him and moan.

"We can't play if you don't trust me, Nat." He skims down my body, taking a nipple into his mouth and sucking until it burns. He continues his descent, tasting, biting, marking me as he does. When he gets to the mound of my covered pussy, he inhales and looks up at me with lust-glazed eyes. "Say you trust me."

Nip.

"No."

"Say it."

Kiss.

"No."

Tearing the thin fabric from my pussy, he swipes his tongue up my slit. Pleasure ripples through me, my toes curling. I flex my calves, causing my ankles to tug on the restraints. It's oddly arousing having them constricted like that.

"Say it." Suck.

"Say it." Lick

"Say it." Bite.

"Yes," I scream, an orgasm pending.

"Yes, what?" he teases.

"Yes, I trust you, you bastard."

I feel his smile against the flesh of my pussy and grip a fistful of his hair, pinning his face there while I grind myself on him, chasing my release.

He allows me to use him as my sex toy for all of two seconds. Gripping my hand, he forces me to release his hair. He pulls back and slides off the side of the bed, dragging my arm above my head and curling the material from the top pillar around my slim wrist. He then brings a new piece of fabric across my body and drapes it over my face.

"Ren," I warn, nervous energy crackling through the air as I breathe against the cool fabric, my sight taken from me.

"Trust me, please." He implores me with his warm tone as he crawls over my body to tie the other wrist to the bedpost.

My chest begins a rapid cadence as I nod in confirmation. *I'll trust him.*

"You're so fucking beautiful. You know that, right?"

My senses are muted by the fabric covering my face, making seeking him out impossible. Anticipation sends a trickle of fear mixed with a huge rush of excitement coursing through my bloodstream, making my skin extra sensitive to any touch.

Hot air caresses over me, and a delicate skim of fingertips traces over me from top to toe, lingering on the places that get a response from my body. His tongue replaces his fingers, exploring, devouring every inch of me. My body is hyper-aware of his touch, the sensation of pleasure amplified by being completely at his mercy.

"I'm going to fuck your pretty little cunt with my tongue, fingers, and then with my hard cock until you're a sopping wet mess."

Shut up and do it, I scream in my mind.

My breathing is making the satin damp, and my head is overheating. I'm dizzy and deliriously aching all over.

Large palms come down on my inner thighs to spread my legs farther apart, yanking on the restraints. Deep, wet plunges of his tongue assault my hole in the most perfect of ways. He fucks me like he needs to. Like my essence is his oxygen.

He feasts on me, sending me over the edge and dragging me back before I can truly take off.

Tease.

Punishing my clit with slaps of his palm and then pinching the delicate flesh between his fingers draws all the blood there. Pulsing, needy aches, driving me fucking crazy before he's back to lapping at me. Sucking the throbbing clit into his mouth, he causes a detonation within me. Desire pools in my lower stomach. My pussy constricts, flooding as pleasure washes through me, robbing me of breath and making my eyes roll to the back of my head.

As I suck for much-needed air, my mouth fills with the silk, depleting me of a full inhale.

His fat dick slaps against my pussy, slipping through the folds, spreading my juices all over himself. And then he's breaching me, his thick mushroom head pushing me past my limit and stretching me to the point of pain. *I love it.* I fucking love it.

His body falls over mine, and then he thrusts forward, filling me up to the hilt.

I feel him everywhere, touching, kissing. Deep strokes touch places never reached before, sending me into oblivion.

Hands tighten on my restrained wrists. He's unrelenting and punishingly rough. Skin slapping skin echoes through the room mixed with his grunts and my screams.

He shows no mercy. And I want none.

He's awakening me to sensations I didn't know possible. Suddenly, his hand comes over my mouth, forcing the fabric down, cutting off my airway.

"Count, sweetness. Five seconds."

His hips piston into me and the pressure of his palm across the satin causes panic and exhilaration all at once. My mind clouds with euphoria, eclipsing everything but the orgasm that rips through me, sending shock waves through every molecule of my body.

When I finally come down, my body is tense all over. I can breathe a little better now that his hand has been removed from my mouth, allowing the silk to dance over my skin with every inhale and exhale. Ren's cock pulls from my body, sending a shiver over me. He crawls up my naked, fevered flesh and grunts as he straddles my shoulders. I can hear him working his own release, and then warm, wet fluid spurts over the fabric draped over my face, dampening it—sticking it to my lips.

"Fuuuckk," he roars, his come still flowing from him. The weight of him is almost suffocating, but I'm too delirious to care about anything but the salty taste of him soaking into my lips.

My limbs are heavy and sore, and every part of me feels the echoes of Ren's touch.

The new day came and went, and we only stopped fucking to eat and sleep.

Ren's soft snores from beside me make a smile creep over my lips. I didn't expect this. *Him.*

It wasn't supposed to go down like this. Yet, I can't force myself to leave. To not want him.

Pulling the covers up over him, I slip from the bed. My mouth is parched, and I'm pretty sure I've burned more calories in the last two days than I have the entire year at the gym. My stomach growls on that thought, demanding fuel. Grabbing a discarded shirt, I drag it over my body and make my way to Ren's kitchen. There's not much in there but a couple of slices of cold leftover pizza that has my name all over it. Plucking a bottle of beer from his stash, I carry my bounty to his couch and collapse on it. The first bite of pizza makes me sigh as I chase it with the beer. I should really get dressed and get back to my own apartment. I have classes tomorrow. But I know I won't.

A buzzing startles me, making me splash myself with beer. *Shit.*

Scrubbing at the mess on Ren's shirt, I seek out the sound of the buzzing. It's coming from Ren's cell phone left on the coffee table. A William is calling. Frowning, I look at the time. Three in the morning. It must be important to be calling so late. I debate waking Ren just as the buzzing stops. Not that important then? A couple of seconds later a text message flashes up.

William: You can't keep leaving me waiting.

William: You're punishing me for what happened to Kate.

My heart speeds up, nearly ripping from my chest at the mention of Kate.

Thud. Thud. Thud.

Guilt douses me. She is the reason I came to Ren. To find the truth—to get justice. And instead, I became just another groupie of Ren Hayes. *I'm a disgrace.*

I stare at the text, reading the little text box visible on his home screen over and over again. My legs wobble as I stand. Unsteadily, I bolt back to the bedroom and flick on the light.

The intrusion of the glow makes Ren groan and pull a pillow over his head. "Need sleep, babe."

Standing over him, I drag the pillow away and show him his phone.

"Who is William?" I demand.

Squinting his eyes up at me, he snatches the phone and reads the messages.

"It's rude to read other people's messages, Nat."

"Don't do that. Tell me who the hell he is and how he knew Kate."

Sighing, he tosses the phone down on the space next to him where I lay moments before, naked and sated. Now I'm running on adrenaline, the blood racing through my veins for very different reasons than the last two nights of pleasure.

"Are you going to sit the fuck down or just hover over me in nothing but my wet shirt?"

Looking down at myself I chew anxiously on my lip and stroke over the wet stain. This gets me a smirk and a raised brow from him.

"Tell me, Ren. I need to know," I snap, refusing to allow that beautiful face to distract me from getting answers.

"You're never going to let this go, are you?" he groans, scrubbing his hands over his face and sitting up.

"Never."

"Fine."

SEVEN

REN

Fuck.

This was a conversation I did not want to have. Not with her. Not with anyone. But after the past couple of days, I know I owe it to her. She lost her best friend. Then, she gave herself to me somewhere along the way as she sought the truth. If I want to keep the girl, I have to tell her.

And fuck do I want to keep her.

I have a waiting list a mile long at the club, and

I'd tell them to scrap it if it meant I got to fuck sweet Natasha every night.

"Ren," she urges, her nostrils flaring.

Running my palm over the back of my neck, I let out a sigh. "It was an accident." I throw on some boxers and sit on the edge of my bed.

"So you've said." Her eyes water and her bottom lip wobbles. I can take her anger, but this fucking sucks.

"Come here," I rumble, reaching for her.

"N-No," she whispers, taking a step away from me. "Just tell me. Please."

"William is my friend from high school," I tell her. "His family..." I inhale the scent of cinnamon and the loss of my mother still makes my chest ache all these years later. "His family paid for my mother's hospital bills when she was diagnosed with cancer. I was a junior in high school. Just seventeen when she passed."

Nat's brows furrow together and I can tell she wants to comfort me, but barely refrains.

"My brother Ronan was twenty and in college. There was no way we could pay the bills. The Warners stepped up, thanks to William, and paid off the debts. Once my brother took off with Harose Records, he paid them back. Every penny. The moment he could. But we never forgot what they did for us."

"I'm sorry about your mom," she murmurs. "But you're beating around the bush. Tell me what happened with Kate."

"I'm getting to that. Anyway, despite our growing apart as far as our careers go, William and I have remained friends. The more he pads his political résumé, the more I don't exactly fit in his world. The past couple of years, he's treated me like a dirty little secret. Normally, I find it funny as fuck and love to taunt him when his proclivities leak over into his pristine politician world." I scrub at my face with my hand that still smells of pussy. "He's into my scene but hides that part of himself. Even from his fiancée. Well, ex-fiancée now."

"William and Kate were seeing each other?" she asks, scrunching her nose. "The note." She leaves the room for a minute and then rushes back in, thrusting the note at me.

***He doesn't love her. She's an accessory to him. I'm real. I know he won't marry her. Not when he has me on the side. I know what he likes because I like it too. It has to be enough*.**

"They were both novices in the whole breathplay kink. And..." I trail off and frown at her. "They fucked up, Nat. Took it too far."

My eyes fall to her throat that is slightly bruised from our own playing. Difference is, I know what the fuck I'm doing. William never should have attempted that shit without getting some training first.

I rise and walk over to Nat. She lifts her chin but doesn't move away. My fingers drag along her throat and I steal a kiss. I don't fucking know if she'll bolt after this and I'll be damned if I don't have her taste on my lips if she does.

"He called me, frantic. Crying. Freaking the fuck out." I cringe as I think of that night. "I showed up, found a scarf around her throat. I couldn't loosen it. I knew she was dead, but performed CPR anyway. It was too late, though. She was gone."

"But it was an accident, so you say. Why didn't he come straight to the police? Why did you cover for him?" she demands, tears welling in her emerald eyes.

"William was worried about his career," I tell her bluntly.

"And what about yours?" Her voice is shrill.

"I owed him. After what he did for Mom..." I stroke her hair from her face and kiss her again. And again. And again. "We can't change what happened. It was an accident. I did what I could to protect my friend. The media would have destroyed him. I couldn't let that happen."

"But Kate?" she sobs.

"I'm sorry," I murmur. "I tried, Nat. I really fucking tried. You were there for the trial. There were no signs of a struggle or rape. She suffocated during sex and it's a fucking tragedy I wish I had the power to undo."

She starts to cry harder. I tug her over to the bed and help her back into it. With her tucked under my arm, I whisper assurances and apologies into her ear as she cries for her friend. And when she's all cried out, she speaks.

"Thank you for telling me."

And she doesn't fucking leave.

***

Two weeks later…

"I need you to do damage control," Ronan growls over the phone. "Xavi is fucking crazy. You signed Berlin Scandal, you can come deal with this psychopath."

I groan as I slip out of my bed. "Not like I wasn't

waiting to get my dick sucked or anything," I bite out as I go on a hunt for some boxers.

"Whatever flavor of the week you have can wait," he grinds out. "This can't."

He hangs up before I have the chance to tell him Natasha isn't a flavor of the week. She's all the flavors. Baskin Robbins—all thirty-one flavors. And my delicious little snack was on her way here from class with a texted promise to suck my damn dick.

Sometimes I hate my brother.

I throw on some jeans as I hear the front door open. Walking over to the doorway, I grab the top of the doorframe and lean into the room, seeking out my fucking girl.

She's distracted by her phone as she tosses her bag and purse down. Most girls wear sexy shit that molds to their skin. Not Nat. Nat wears jeans and hoodies and her cute-as-fuck glasses. Her hair is always in wild, blond disarray. She wears the same worn tennis shoes every damn day. But goddamn is she hot. Helluva lot hotter than any of the women I've ever taken to bed with me.

"Did you miss me?" she asks, shooting her gaze over to me for the first time tonight. Her green eyes twinkle with lust as she takes in my bare chest. "I missed you."

I chuckle as I release the doorframe and saunter over to her. She wraps her arms around my middle as I kiss her deeply. If two weeks ago someone had told me I'd fuck a girl and never want her to leave, I would've laughed. But that's exactly what happened. For two weeks straight, we've spent every free moment together.

And the club?

I cleared that schedule because I have something better.

Her fingers find my jeans and she unzips them before diving her hand into my boxers. I groan as she squeezes me.

"I have to leave," I grumble against her hair and then kiss her head. "I don't have time for one of your sexy, teasing blowjobs."

She lifts her head and pouts at me. "You're not going to the club, are you?"

"Why?" I taunt. "Would you be jealous?"

Her eyes roll. "Don't be gross."

Chuckling, I shrug. "Yeah, I guess a lot of those people there are gross. You know I don't need the club when I have your sweet little body in my bed each night."

She grins triumphantly at me. "Well, since you

have to go, I guess you don't get to see my new bra and panties."

I grab the hem of her hoodie, yanking it up over her head. Raking my gaze over the swells of her breasts, I appreciate the way the black, lacy fabric holds her perfect tits in the sexiest of ways. "I have time to take a peek."

A cute laugh escapes her. "A peek always ends with you seeing everything."

Smirking at her, I undo her jeans and then push them down her thighs. Her panties match and are sexy as fuck. I bear hug her and carry her squealing ass over to the couch. She whines when I bend her over the back. I give her ass a good swat that makes her yelp before I shove my boxers and jeans down my thighs. Reaching between her thighs, I seek out her clit over her lacy panties. She moans and pushes her butt toward me. Nat is easy to please. Her body is so fucking responsive. I work her hard and fast, knowing I'm pressed for time, until she's crying out. The moment she's shuddering with her orgasm, I tug her panties to the side and slide into her tight heat.

"Ren!" she cries out, clenching her cunt around my dick. "Whaaaa!"

Whatever the fuck she was going to say gets cut

off when I slam into her hard. I drive into her relentlessly, our bodies slapping loudly. I take pleasure in slapping her ass over her panties because each time I do, she tightens around my dick. Pressing on her back, I flatten her against the cushions, no doubt making it difficult for her to breathe as her face is forced into the fabric. With her ass prone to me, I fuck her hard. From this angle, I know I'm hitting all the sweet spots inside her. Her muffled cry is my only warning that she's coming again. My cock seems to get sucked deep into her black hole of fucking pleasure. I come with a guttural groan, releasing into her, hot and furious. It isn't until my dick stops twitching that I realize I forgot to wrap my fucking dick up.

"Shit," I hiss, yanking out of her.

Cum runs down her inner thigh. Jesus. So fucking hot. And reckless! I'm not reckless. Not with women. Not with sex. I am careful. Fuck.

"I'm clean," I choke out, frowning down at my seed seeping from her.

"I'm clean too," she squeaks out, standing up. "It's okay." Her cheeks burn bright red with shame. Fuck that.

"Come here," I demand, pulling her to me. "I'm sorry."

She stands on her toes and kisses me. "Apology accepted. Do you really have to go?"

"Yeah. Crisis at Harose."

"I have homework anyway," she says, pulling up her jeans. "Wake me up when you get home."

I twist a strand of her blond hair around my finger and tug. "Oh, I will, sweetheart." I grin wolfishly at her. "You still owe me a blowjob."

EIGHT

NATASHA

After grabbing a snack and finishing up some assignments due for school, I take a nap, knowing Ren will wake me up with his tongue when he arrives home.

The past couple of weeks have been the best in my life. I spend most days on schoolwork and every night in a state of bliss. He was unexpected, and we were brought together in the most unconventional of ways. But it feels right. Like I'm supposed to be right here with him.

The sun has set, and the room is shrouded in darkness when I arise from hearing the front door closing. I don't move, instead wait, holding my breath with anticipation. It's only been a couple of hours, and I spent one of those sleeping, but I miss him even in sleep. *Pathetic*.

A silhouette fills the doorway—seconds pass and my heart rate spikes.

The presence in the room feels different, and it doesn't bring with it the intense longing Ren draws out of me, instead, an ominous chill drapes over my body, blanketing me in unease. Sitting up abruptly when I hear footsteps move across the hardwood floor, a gasp shoots from my lungs and fear trickles into my bloodstream upon realization the form is not Ren's. I scoot back on the bed until I'm pinned against the headboard. The shadow stalks across the room, stopping at the foot of the bed.

"Who are you?" we both speak in unison.

His voice is curious, bewildered even. It's not smooth, confident like Ren. And my own is hurried, nervous.

Reaching across the bed, I flick on the lamp to find a well-presented man suited and booted. Blond hair swept neatly across his head, blue eyes gazing down at me.

There's something off with the way his eyes zone in on the faint marks left on my neck from Ren. *Hunger.*

"Ren doesn't usually bring women here." He frowns. His tongue sweeps out to moisten his lips as he surveys me.

"He made an exception," I grind out, irritated that he assumes I'm some groupie. "Who are you?" He makes me uncomfortable. I don't care if he does know Ren. Who just wanders into someone's bedroom?

"Oh, forgive me, I'm a friend of Ren's. I was invited here," he tells me, and then a grin pulls up his lip. Greedy blue eyes scan down my body that's only covered with an old tee of Ren's. My legs are bare, gaining his attention. "He left you here for me?" he suddenly announces, a light seemingly going off in his mind. Smirking, he slips out of his jacket and loosens his tie.

No, he fucking didn't.

Sliding out of the bed, I rush over to where I left my jeans draped over a chair and shove them up my legs.

"What are you doing?" he asks, confused.

"Listen, eh...?"

"William," he finishes for me, sending a wave of

nausea swirling in my stomach.

"William?" I breathe. I'm so frozen in shock by the turn of events it takes me a second to realize he's advanced across the room and is only a couple of feet from me.

"Your bruises are so pretty. Let me darken them for you," he murmurs, reaching out to touch me, making me jerk backward in response.

"Don't touch me," I snap.

Narrowing his baby blues on me, he takes a step forward. "Don't play coy, honey, it's unbecoming."

Thud, thud, thud.

How could Ren invite him here with no warning —with not being here? *He set you up.*

No way. He wouldn't. I haven't imagined these past two weeks. The way he touches me. Looks at me. That's not fake. That's not been lies. *He charms people.*

No. *Makes you see what you want.*

No. *He's a liar.*

No. No. No.

William grabs at me, his large palms clammy on my skin. Without thought, my knee jerks upright, straight into his crotch. Howling in pain, he hunches over, grabbing his junk.

"You fucking bitch," he growls. I move past him

to grab my shoes and purse and flee. I need to get out of here. To think—to plan—to decide what I'm going to do about Ren. And about William.

NINE

REN

"They're fresh, unique. The market needs a band like this." I yawn, rubbing a hand down my face. I'm bored with this and want to get back to Nat. She fucking consumes my every thought. The little fucking minx is intoxicating.

"It doesn't matter if they're going to be a nightmare to manage." Ronan's jaw tightens and his eyes narrow on me.

After convincing the lead singer of Berlin Scandal to jot his fucking name on the dotted line, my brother's been giving me grief. He doesn't do divas unless they're young, naïve, and calling him daddy. Xavi wasn't being a diva per se, he just wanted to make sure they weren't getting screwed over. The music industry has changed over the years, and artists have a lot more power than they used to. They have a lot more say in the music they produce. That's the company my brother wanted to make, and we're a standout label for that reason. We want the talent to be involved in every step of their career. If they're happy and making music, the audience will believe in them and the money will come with them. Win-win.

"If he turns out to be a problem, you're fucking fixing said problem." He groans, sipping whiskey from a tumbler. If we didn't share the same dark eyes, you'd never know we are related. We couldn't be more opposite, but we're a team. And family. He trusts me, and that's why we work—why Harose works.

Where I'm all visible tattoos and bad boy persona, Ronan is a suit with a no-nonsense attitude. People take him seriously. He's stern and bossy and an overall dick when he wants to be. His suits are expensive and his business sense is spot-on. People don't fuck with my brother for fear of getting sent to the goddamn corner or getting an ass whipping.

"We done?" I ask, my ass bouncing in the seat, desperate to get back to Nat.

"You got somewhere to be?" he mocks, raising a brow.

"I do. Asshole." I grin as I stand and slip on my jacket.

"What the fuck's going on with you?" he asks, sitting forward to study me like he can read the answers to his question on my face. It reminds me of a time when he was responsible for my wellbeing. When I'd fuck around at school and he'd hand my ass to me like he was my damn father. Three years. We're three years apart, but ever since Mom got sick, he stepped into a parental role that he never left. Eighteen came and went. Ronan is still a bossy, nosy dick.

"What do you mean?" I play aloof because I don't know what's going on with me. I've never felt like this about a woman before.

"You're acting differently. What is it that you're in a hurry to get back to or should I say with whom?"

Damn. Am I that transparent?

"Spill it, little brother," he orders. "Who the hell

has snared the legendary pussy pleaser, Ren fucking Hayes?"

Sighing, I run a hand through my hair and shrug. "It's new. She's new, refreshing. Fucking exquisite." I chuckle, conjuring up her beautiful form in my mind. Her curves, the little dimples at the base of her spine. The birthmark that almost resembles a star in her inner thigh. Her giggle when I touch her sides where she's ticklish. Fuck, the way she gasps for air when I restrict her pretty little mouth.

A slapping of Ronan's hand hitting his knee drags me from my thoughts. "You fucking love this girl." It's a statement, not a question—a wrong one.

"Shut up. I wouldn't know how to love a girl like her or any fucking woman."

You fucking love this girl.

It's been two weeks. No one falls in love that fast. *But I've been eyeing her since the trial.* I don't love her. *Denial.*

"Ren, I've never seen you like this."

"Like what?" I snap, picking up a pen from his desk and tossing it at him.

Chuckling, he shakes his head and props one leg up, resting his ankle on his knee as he leans back in his leather chair. "My baby brother is in love."

Before I can answer or throw something bigger at

him, the door opens and his flavor of the month walks in and stops in her tracks when she sees me in here. Her eyes widen and go between the two of us.

"Oops sorry, *Daddy*." She bites on her finger and twirls her hair with the other hand. "I forgot to knock." Her tone is soft and innocent, but her eyes scream anything but.

"You're a bad girl, Starla," my brother growls. "You know the rules."

Her cheeks flush, and I roll my eyes. Can't they save this shit for when I'm not here?

"I do," she replies, her voice breathless. "I deserve a spanking."

Rising to his feet and moving around his desk, Ronan ushers me to the door with a firm hand on my shoulder. "Duty calls, brother. But we will revisit this conversation."

Like fuck, we will. I hear the swat he gives her ass as the door swings closed on my exit.

I shoot a text to Nat to ask if she wants me to pick up food on the way home but get no reply. I don't even want to dissect this shit Ronan was spouting. I will admit I care about Nat. Damn, she worked her way into my *give a shit book* when she relentlessly stalked me and gave me hell at every turn. But love?

My phone buzzes with an incoming text and my chest gets a weird fucking exciting thrill pounding in it. *It's not fucking love.*

I stare at the screen and scowl. It's not Nat, it's fucking William.

William: Where are you? We were supposed to meet tonight.

Fuck. I forgot about him and that he asked to meet up tonight. I didn't say for sure that we could. I've been blowing him off for fucking months because I still struggle with what happened with Kate. If I killed a girl, I'd not be eager to get back to the scene, to playing, but William is like a drug addict after a fix. He's been relentless in his pleas to take him to the club, to let him join me in a session. I shoot back a reply and toss my cell in the passenger seat.

Me: Can't tonight. I have work.

"Nat, wake up, beautiful. I brought food," I call out as I push through the front door grinning, knowing how much she loves junk food.

The place is quiet. No lights are on, but a warm glow is seeping from the bedroom doorway.

"Nat?" I call, trotting inside to see the bed a mess but no Nat. Her sweatshirt is dumped on the end of the bed, but she's nowhere.

I pull out my cell and try her number. It rings and then goes to voicemail. *What the fuck?* I shoot her a text.

Me: Where did you go? I brought dinner and planned to eat your sweet pussy for dessert. P.S. You still owe me a blowjob.

I collapse on the couch with the pizza I brought home and flick on an old episode of *Game of Thrones*. Damn, that dragon bitch reminds me of Nat. From a passive little princess into a badass dragon riding queen. I'm about to pull my dick out and rub one out when my cell dings.

A middle finger emoji followed with a text.

Nat: Blow this.

What the fuck?

Me: You're acting like a brat. What the hell is your problem?

Nothing.

Has she gone crazy? Is this because I bailed to go sort shit out for work? Is this a relationship?

My head swims with confusion and a million questions. Fuck this. Abandoning the pizza, I grab my car keys and drive to her shitty apartment.

It's fucking cold and damp by the time I get there. The clock reads 1:13 on my dash and I debate turning around and going back home. Since when the fuck did I become this guy?

The type running around after a woman.

Since her.

Turning the car off, I slip out and look up to see her lights on. I'm going to demand she stop being a diva and let me fuck her tight little cunt into a frenzy. Then she can get on her knees and beg for forgiveness for being a pissy bitch. I need to set the ground rules now if we're going to keep this up—whatever the fuck *this* is.

The elevator is broken in her building, so I have to climb the three flights of stairs. She owes me for this crap. I ring her bell and step from foot to foot, trying to warm the fuck up.

"Nat, open the fucking door. I know you're in there," I grind out. She's taking this too far.

The door flies open, and a seething firecracker glares at me. *Dragon queen.*

"So I worked later than I thought. You can't just leave and have a tantrum." I smile, lifting a brow at her. But she doesn't smile back. Her posture is rigid, her lips pursed. Red swollen eyes make the green look piercing. "Nat?" I frown.

"This"—she waves a finger between us—"is done."

"Done? Not happening, Nat. Stop being a brat," I growl. I'm getting pissed off standing in the hallway arguing about bullshit with a chick I want to throttle not just for pleasure right now.

"I'm not a brat. You're a fucking asshole."

She's like a different fucking person. Something's crawled inside her and turned my nerdy, little beauty into a head case. "I was working. You're being insane. Call me when you stop whatever the fuck this is." I scoff, turning to leave. There's only so much bullshit I'll take from her ass.

She shoves me, palms flat on my back and all her might thrown into it. I don't fucking budge, but she tried. Turning, I narrow my eyes on her.

"You think this is because you had to work? This is because you're a fucking liar," she screeches.

Grabbing her wrist when her hands come up to shove me again, I back her into her apartment and shove the door closed with a kick of my boot.

"Get out," she barks.

"Not a chance," I bite back. "You're going to tell me what the hell has crawled up your ass."

She glowers at me. "I met your *friend* tonight."

I rack my brain. No women know where I live, so this can't be because of a woman.

"William," she barks out, seeing me struggling.

My jaw tightens and my stomach twists.

"Did he do something to you?" I ask, closing in on her, dragging my eyes over every inch of her to see if she's hurt. He's dead.

A weird wretch comes from her, startling me. "Why would you ask that? You said he was harmless, decent."

"Nat, just fucking answer my question. Did he do something?" *He wouldn't...*

"He turned up at your place. I was in bed waiting for you."

I'm going to fucking vomit. I swear to God if he touched her, I'll be found guilty because this time I will be.

"Did you leave me there for him?" she sobs, wrapping her arms around her waist.

My heart fucking drops like stone.

"What? No, no way. Why would you think that?" I try to move closer to her, because all I want to do is hold her—comfort her—own her. But she steps back and holds a hand up to stop me. I'm going to kill that motherfucker. I forgot I gave him a key ages ago. He bitched about having to wait outside for me in view of the public one time. Fucking dickhead thinks he's more recognizable than he is.

"He said you left me there for him. Why the hell would you invite him there? Do you know how painful it was for me meeting him like that? The man who killed Kate?"

My body deflates like a lead balloon. She's right. And I'm an asshole.

"I'm sorry. He shouldn't have gone there. Wires got crossed. It was a mistake."

Her beautiful face contorts in anger. "Just another mistake? Your accidents have consequences, Ren. I can't believe I trusted you and let you manipulate me into sharing your bed."

"That's not fair," I snarl.

"No, what's not fair is being left by you to wake up to my best friend's killer asking to put bruises on me." Her chest rises and falls with her rage building. "What's not fair is for him to think it's normal that he was meeting you and found a woman instead. Is that how it works, Ren? You work the women in and then when you're done, you offer them to him?"

I would never offer her to him. Never. She's fucking mine.

"Don't say that shit," I growl. "You're angry, baby, I get it. But don't make up some fucking crazy-ass story in your head to make me the villain again. I would kill William if he ever touched you. Or hurt another woman. I'm not the monster you're trying to paint me as to alleviate the guilt you feel for wanting me. For wanting us. For loving what we've become."

Her entire torso shakes with her bitter laugh. "Don't flatter yourself. We don't have anything. You were a good fuck. A fling. A dance on the wild side. Nothing more. And we're done."

"Don't do this."

"Get out." She points her finger to the door.

"Nat, don't fucking do this."

"GET OUT."

She's shaking from head to fucking toe. I don't want to leave her in this state, but I'm doing more harm than good being here. She has demons running wild in her mind and I can't make her see that I'm not the man she convinced herself I was.

I'd never hurt her.

I'd never fucking hurt her.

I love her.

Fuck, I love her...

"Please just go, get out, get out, get out," she screams, her tiny fist pounding against my chest.

I surrender. Against every part of me telling me to grab her and never let go I turn and leave.

TEN

NATASHA

A ***week and a half later…***

I stare at the last text Ren sent me earlier today, hating the aching loneliness in my chest. *Stop it, Nat.* He's a dirty bastard. Chewing on my bottom lip, I consider messaging him. But what would I say?

I hate that you let your horrible friend who accidentally killed my best friend find me in bed and threaten to do creepy shit to me, but I like your dick so it's okay?

And your smile...

And your laugh...

And the way your eyes grow serious as you brush the hair from my eyes right before you kiss me...

Tears well in my eyes and I quickly blink them away. I like him for way more than his dick and it sucks. It sucks that I can't just write him out of my life. To move the hell on. I've been obsessing over Ren Hayes—albeit in a hateful way at first—for over six months. Following his every move on social media. So when we fell into whatever whirlwind we've landed in, it happened fast. It was intense and vivid and real. And that's why it hurts so much. He's more than a nice dick and finesse in the bedroom.

We had something good going.

Or so I thought.

I read his text again.

Ren: I miss your stalking. I'll be at Ritz Russo's. Friday night is Talent Night. Fresh meat. I could use a sidekick.

This is the hardest part. He keeps texting me. Being his normal sweet and sexy self. And it's hard to undo the two perfect weeks we had in my mind. A girl can only get off so many times with a vibrator and a memory before she starts to physically ache for the real thing.

I start to reply to him. Something angry and

mean. Just like all the rest that won't deter him. In the end, I stupidly tell him the truth.

Me: I miss the time we had together. I miss you. But, Ren, that's my problem. I shouldn't miss you or want you.

Or love you.

Ren: I see what you're doing…

Me: What's that?

Ren: Pushing me away.

Me: I already did that. You're away.

Ren: No, I'm giving you your space, but I'm not done with you, Natasha. I don't think I'll ever be. It used to freak me the fuck out. Not anymore.

My heart does a little patter that has me growling in annoyance.

Ren: It makes me want to try harder. For the record, I've never had to try this hard to get the girl. But rest assured, I'm trying really fucking hard. And. I. Will. Get. The. Girl. Break time is over.

I'm trying hard to fight a smile. Smiling is definitely the exact opposite of what I should be doing. I should be scowling and cursing him. But the girl inside of me who fell hard for this boy—she's on cloud nine. She wants the boy to get her.

Something catches my eye and I slouch down in the driver's seat of my car. Bingo. I've been staking out William Warner's office this week—it didn't take long to find his Facebook profile through Ren's friend list. Within minutes, I had all kinds of information about him. Even took a peek at his ex-pretty fiancée. Although, on her social media, she shows she's in a "complicated" relationship and he's not her friend.

He climbs into his Mercedes and pulls out of the spot. Slowly, I drive after him. His journey is short, heading straight to a familiar place. Hush. The same place where Ren touched me for the first time. When I let him, knowing full well he was my enemy.

William is in a hurry and has done a wardrobe change in the car along the way. He's missing his suit jacket and he's wearing a ball cap. If he thinks he's blending in, he's not. No one wears a ball cap with dress clothes. I climb out and trail after him. Having been here before, I know the drill. I use my membership card and slip inside. Once my card is tucked in my pocket, I pull out my phone. I start a recording just in case. You can never be too careful with people like William—especially given what I know now.

I want to hear it from his lips. That he killed

Kate. Accident, maybe, but I need to hear his account for that night's events. And I need to know if he feels remorse. I'll never be able to close this chapter in my life otherwise.

William walks over to the bar, orders a drink, and then heads for one of the main rooms. Where Ren was in a private room with that skank last time I was here, William seems to be on a hunt first. A chill slides down my spine. He lifts his head, searching the crowd, and I freeze.

Two black eyes and a bandage over his nose.

Ouch.

Fucker deserved whatever happened to him.

The pulse of the music and buzz of the crowd causes me to lose him. I wander around aimlessly until someone grabs a fistful of my hoodie from behind and pulls me back. Hot breath tickles my ear.

"Must be fate," William says over the music. "I found you at Ren's place and now you found me at Ren's favorite hangout." His palm slides around to my front, openly groping my breast in front of all the drunk people around us. "You're too late, gorgeous. He's already slipped away with a sloppy skank. But don't worry, *I* can satisfy you."

I tense, biting back my words. Ren's at Ritz

Russo's, not here. William is a liar, I'm learning. What else has he lied about?

Kate's sweet face springs in my mind, spurring me into action. "Can we talk somewhere private?"

William presses his mediocre erection against my ass. "I'll lead the way."

The urge to call Ren is strong. And the thought that he's my go-to person is even more surprising.

William walks me down a corridor and then into a small room. A man sits at a desk, tapping away at a computer.

"We need a room," William says lowly. "Ren Hayes will okay it. I'm his friend William."

I wince. How can Ren be friends with this douchebag?

The man at the desk jolts at the name, staring at William with narrowed eyes. His jaw ticks as he studies William and then cuts his eyes to me. I attempt to keep my features impassive, but my lip wobbles slightly. I'm willingly going into a room alone with the guy who killed my best friend. This is stupid. Stupid but necessary for answers.

The man tears his stare from me and makes a phone call.

"Mr. Hayes," the man says. "Sorry to bother you, but I have a William here with a lovely blond lady.

He's asking to use a private room under your name."

The man nods. "Yes. Of course. Thank you, sir."

He hangs up and stands. "Welcome," he says to us both. "Mr. Hayes said you can use the Blue Box. It's small and quiet. Very private."

William nods like a bobble head. "Perfect. I knew he'd come through."

My stomach drops to my feet—a pebble forms in my throat. Ren wouldn't so easily let this bastard take a girl to a room, would he? And using his name? Surely not after everything he's been through with this guy.

My mind flitters with all the memories of our time together. When I told him William came to his house with me there, he was horrified. He promised he would never allow what happened with Kate to happen to someone else. And although I reacted in anger at first, I believe him. A sense of calm washes over me. Ren was so sure of the fact he'd protect me. That he'd find me. The fact William just told him our whereabouts is comforting. Ren has a trick up his sleeve and I need to trust in what he said. That I'm not alone. That he wants to protect me. Even when I've pushed him away and told him I hated him.

I don't hate him.

I can't stop thinking about him. I can't stop reminiscing over our time together. I can't stop dreaming about the way he took care of my body or how he took care of me.

We follow the man down a series of hallways. He unlocks a door and a blue light shines out into the hallway. From my vantage point, I can tell it's indeed small, with no obvious cameras like the other room, but Ren said they have them for safety clauses. So I can only hope they're in here but out of sight. The room is no bigger than fifteen by fifteen feet with a small bed in the center. Simple and to the point.

"Enjoy your evening," the man says, turning on his heel.

Before he's rounded the corner, William gives me a shove into the room. I stumble until my knees hit the bed. Rather than falling and putting myself in a vulnerable position, I spin around and square off with him. He closes the door and is already tugging off his tie.

"You killed Kate," I blurt out, meeting his stare bravely.

Panic flashes in his eyes and he frowns, freezing in place. "Ren told you?"

"I pieced together most of it," I tell him. "I'm sorry the prosecuting attorneys didn't pick up on it."

I glare at him. "For some reason, Kate was in love with you."

He scoffs. "Hardly."

"She thought you should leave your fiancée for her." I tear up with emotion. "But you killed her instead."

"Enough," he barks out, giving me a shove.

I hit the bed and bounce. Before I can scramble away, he flips me over. A scream is lodged in my throat as I ready myself to fight against a sexual attack, but he's not trying to rip off my jeans. He's pulling my phone out of my pocket.

No!

"Recording me, huh?" he demands. "Bad girl."

My phone hits the floor with a sickening crack.

"William, I just came here for answers. I want to know why you killed my friend!"

With quick movements, he slides his necktie around my throat and yanks back, hauling me off the bed. I claw at the tie, but he twists the material, cutting off my air supply.

One.

Two.

Three.

Don't panic.

Four.

Five.

Six.

Fuck.

Seven.

Blackness eats at my vision.

Screw this asshole.

Slamming my foot down hard on his dress shoe, I revel in the howl of pain that escapes him. As soon as he loosens his grip, I kick away from him, thrilled when I nail him in the nuts. He falls onto the bed whimpering, holding his balls.

"Tell me everything and don't miss a single detail," I hiss through my tears.

"Your phone is dead. You won't have leverage on me."

Does he not know about the cameras or does he just think he can buy the footage from whomever is recording? *Please be recording.*

I hate entitled assholes like him. They think they're above retribution—above the law and decency. Williams of the world are why it's so broken.

"I just want to know the truth. Tell me the damn truth."

ELEVEN

REN

Come the fuck on.

I hit every red light from Ritz Russo's—where I had my eye on a new singer who had a whole Halsey vibe going on—to Hush. Luckily, when I pull up out front, one of the usual valet guys sees me right away. I toss my keys at him and then bolt inside. Pushing past horny fuckers everywhere, I make it down to reception where Jonas waits at his desk with a frown on his face.

"Everything okay?"

"He hasn't hurt her," he assures me, nodding toward his laptop where he's no doubt watching the cameras.

"Good. Thanks for calling me."

Jonas was under strict instruction to not allow William into any rooms without my supervision, ever since what went down with Kate. But knowing Nat would be sniffing him out, eager for answers, I told him to be especially aware of any weird requests. The moment he called to tell me William had a blonde with him, I was already on my way.

I promised her he'd never hurt her. Never hurt anyone ever again and I meant it.

I fucking threatened William from ever touching her again, or even inhaling the same air.

Him walking into my place was one thing. But creeping on her in my room? Then saying the shit he did? Not cool. When the dickhead got lippy with me, I saw red. Rammed my fist right into his pretty Ken doll face. It satisfies me knowing his face is all fucked up.

Bottom line is, we've moved on.

The Warners helped when we needed it, but William has used that piece of leverage over me for a long time. I let him, too. It wasn't until Natasha showed up and he fucked with her that my "we go way back" fog began to clear. I told him he needed to back the hell off this scene and me. And especially Nat.

I thought we had an agreement.

Yet, here we are.

Me hauling ass to the Blue Box. The room is outfitted with hidden cameras. So at least if he hurt my girl, we'd know about it. When I reach the room, I hear yelling. Not wasting a second, I burst inside. I expect something horrible like him forcing himself on her.

Not this.

Not Natasha looking like a fierce angel, both hands fisted, as she yells at William. He's on the bed, curled into a ball moaning about his bruised nuts.

Good girl.

Good fucking girl.

"Say it," she cries out, hitting him with her fists wherever she can land a punch.

"I killed her, okay?" he whimpers.

Her shoulders hunch. "Did she fight? Did you try to save her?"

"She always fought," he mutters. "It was part of the excitement. I guess...I mean, I always got turned on by her fighting. We both did."

"Did you try to save her?"

"Of course I tried to fucking save her," he snaps at her. "Do you think it looks good on me to be associated with a bitch I choked to death?"

Nat starts pummeling him again as she sobs. "She was an amazing person! You ruined her and couldn't even save her! You let Ren take the fall so your precious popularity would be intact! I hate you!"

Stalking over to her, I pull her back and into my arms. With a kiss to the top of her head, I silently assure her I've got her. She turns and hugs me, crying into my chest.

"It's okay, baby," I croon, stroking my hands through her hair. "We're together now and I've got you."

William sits up on the bed and glowers at me. "So it's like that, man? You're choosing sides and picking this crazy bitch? What about everything I did for you, Ren? With Rose?"

I stiffen. "My mother has nothing to do with this. Your dad helped us when we needed it, but we long since paid that debt. I owe you nothing, William. I thought we could be friends, but you're too far gone. You're like all the other politicians—sick, corrupt, evil."

He sneers at me. "It's like that? Well, maybe I

should march my ass down to the police department and show them what you did to my face." As if Ronan's best friend—and cop—Blaine would do anything besides laugh cruelly at him. William has no idea that he's not the only connected person in this city. We passed the Warners up on influence years ago.

Natasha hugs me tighter, which spurs me on.

"You can fucking try. And we'll tell them who's really responsible for Kate's death. Accident or not, that can't look good for your public image," I threaten.

He laughs, cold and cruel. "I destroyed her phone. There is no evidence."

"You must be ten kinds of stupid if you think I'd willingly let you go into a room alone with my fucking girl and not have some sort of insurance in place. This room has cameras. They all do, asshole. It's how we protect everyone here from violence. And accidents," I growl. "Your little confession is mine."

His mouth gapes open. "B-But...Ren! You can't do this to me! You'll ruin me."

Ignoring him, I grip Nat's face in my hands, tilting her head up. "What do you want me to do, baby?"

She smiles up at me. "I don't want him anywhere near you or me."

"Done," I say and then lift a brow for her to continue.

"I want to save this information for a rainy day. Right now, it doesn't change the outcome. Kate's still dead." Her bottom lip wobbles slightly. "But, it will keep his ass on a short leash—one we'll be holding."

"This is ridiculous," William snarls.

I pin him with a hard glare. "I want you to get the hell out of Hush, William. You're not welcome here anymore. Consider yourself officially banned. And if I ever find out you so much as consider putting your hand around another person's throat, I will destroy you. This recording will be anonymously sent to every news outlet and the police. Are we clear?"

"This is blackmail," he bites back. "You can go to jail for that."

"Are we playing chicken now?" I ask, gripping Nat's shoulders to move her aside so I can walk over to where William sits on the bed. I snag the front of his dress shirt and haul him to his feet so we're face-to-face. "Let's play, motherfucker. We'll see who's the goddamn chicken."

His eyes widen with fear. Good. Let him be

scared of me. My blackmailing him will pale in comparison with him hiding his own truths from the world. I know this dick. I've known him for a long time. He's a pussy and will fold.

"Fine," he snaps. "Just leave me the hell alone."

He grabs his tie from the floor and storms off. As soon as he's gone, I pick up Nat's smashed phone and frown. "I'm sorry about this," I tell her, turning to look at her.

Before I get a chance to say another word, she flies into my arms, knocking me against the wall behind me. Her fingers dive into my hair as her lips crash to mine. She locks her legs around my waist, hooking herself to me like a monkey on a tree. I kiss her deeply and desperately. I've missed her. This. Us. I miss the way she makes my heart beat faster and my cock throb harder. I miss her voice and her taste and her motherfucking scent. Barely, I manage to lock the door. I'm about to rip off her shirt when I remember the cameras.

"Wait," I growl, nodding my head over to the wall. "We're being watched."

"By the receptionist?"

"For now, but there are people who pay to watch others. Voyeurism is a kink here at Hush. I'll have Jonas crop out the confession," I assure her. "And this, too. I just want you to know Jonas may get an eyeful."

"What happens if you don't crop this out?" she murmurs, sliding to her feet and stepping back. She pulls her hoodie up over her head before dropping it. Her white bra glows under the blue lights.

"Then those paying customers will see," I growl, my dick turning to stone.

"Will they see this?" she murmurs, undoing her bra from the back and dropping it to the floor. Her full tits are on full display. Fucking. Naughty. Girl.

I rip off my Henley and toss it away. "They'll see the way I fuck you so hard you scream." I unbuckle my jeans and send them to the floor before palming my aching cock through my boxers. "They'll see how hard I get from just looking at you."

She bites on her bottom lip, feigning innocence. But lust burning in her eyes gives away her true intent. She's a kinky girl. Natasha is every bit into this as I am. "Will they see how wet you make me?" she purrs, pushing down her jeans and panties. I lick my lips when she kicks off her shoes and steps out of her clothes. In nothing but her socks, she looks good enough to eat.

I shove down my boxers and step out of my own clothes and shoes. Prowling toward her, I love the gleam of wickedness in her eyes. I snag an arm around her waist before throwing us onto the bed together. Our mouths meet in a heated frenzy. Fuck, I've missed her so bad. She whimpers when I rub against her clit, desperate to be inside her.

"Ren," she moans. "Stop teasing me."

"Tell me you're sorry," I tease. "Tell me you're sorry for denying me what we both want." I slightly press the tip of my dick against her slick opening. "Tell me, Nat, and I'll give you what you're begging for."

"I'm sorry," she breathes. "I'm sorry for denying us. We're good together. So good."

Grinning, I drive into her with one hard thrust that makes her scream. I nip at her lip and tweak her nipple with my fingers as I grind into her. We wiggle ourselves into an angle that has me rubbing against her clit as I rock and circle my hips. My piercing rubs her in just the right way because she claws at me each time I hit the good spots. It feels fucking amazing being with her. Her cunt is wet and hot and tight as hell. Each time I pull out, it seems to suck me back into her.

"Ren!" she cries out as she nears the edge of bliss.

"That's it," I rumble. "Get your pussy nice and juicy for me. It feels so good for me, baby. I want to feel your cunt clenching around me. Make me come, beautiful. I want to fill you the fuck up."

She groans and then her breasts thrust upward as she gives in to her climax. My name is shouted from her lips, echoing off the walls around us. Just knowing someone will be watching later, their breathing hitching the moment she comes, has me hissing in ecstasy. I rock my hips against her as my dick throbs out my release. Fucking her bare and filing her with my cum has got to be one of the hottest things I've ever done. With anyone else it would feel reckless and stupid.

With Nat?

It feels right.

Like one day, I'll fill her up just right and she'll wake up one day carrying my fucking kid. My dick jolts within her. When my eyes drag to her hooded ones, I press a small kiss to her lips.

"I make you happy," she says, her voice in awe.

"You have no idea," I murmur. "You make me want things I've never wanted out of life before."

"Like?"

"Like more." Marriage. Kids. House. Dog. The whole goddamn package. "So much more, baby."

"I want more too," she breathes. "I'm sorry I left you. I won't leave you again."

"Aww," I tease, nipping at her bottom lip. "Don't give up so easily. I'd love for you to try. Then, I can tie your pretty ass to my bed again." I grin devilishly at her. "Are you going to try and leave?"

"I'll try..." She smirks. "If you think you can catch me."

Grabbing her wrists, I pin them to the bed. I collect them both in one hand and slide the other to her throat. My dick has begun to harden again—always fucking eager with her—and I begin a slow, rocking dance with my hips.

"Ten," I tell her, giving her throat a small squeeze.

She nods, lust twinkling in her eyes. "Ten."

One.

Two.

Kiss her pouty lips.

Three.

Four.

Squeeze tighter. Revel in the hiss of air trying to claw its way down her throat and into her lungs.

Five.

Six.

Admire the dark shade of purple her face turns, especially under the blue lights.

Seven.

Eight.

Grind against her sensitive clit.

Nine.

Ten.

Breathe.

She moans when I release her neck, sucking in a gulp of air before exhaling a delicious word. "Again, Ren. Choke me. I love it."

I fuck her slowly, smiling against her lips. "Eleven."

"Eleven."

One.

Two.

Three...

I'm never going to grow tired of this girl. Fucking never.

She's mine.

She always will be.

EPILOGUE

REN

Two months later…

"Her," I say, pointing to a brunette standing next to the bar owner. "The one standing next to the guy with the lip ring behind the bar."

Nat squints through the crowd, searching her out. "Oh! I see her. She's singing tonight? Really that good?"

So fucking good.

Ronan will lose his mind when he hears how good she is. This chick has the sultry, sexy voice of someone like Halsey, but then belts out the higher notes with a slight rock and roll scream like that of Bishop Briggs. Her range is wide, which will convert on stage well. Radio stations will love her voice. Sometimes I have a really good fucking feeling. With this chick, I almost feel the buzz in my veins. Her success is untapped, but like that of a gold mine. We just need to get her to Harose. Snatch her up before someone else does.

"Just wait," I assure Nat. "You'll be blown away."

When the bar owner catches me staring at the girl, he glowers at me. The guy looks like he's the type who loves to throw punches. Tattoos crawl up his neck, sharply ending at his jawline. His dark brown hair is short on the sides and styled to look messy on top of his head. The scruff on his cheeks looks badass, reminding me of how Ronan keeps his. This guy, though, is the opposite of my brother. All black clothes and a black fucking attitude. I throw a grin his way.

I don't want your fucking girlfriend, is the look I give him.

I have my own.

Wrapping my arms around Nat, I kiss the top of her head and rock with her as she moves to the music blasting from the speakers. When she rubs her ass against me, it makes me want to take her right here in front of everyone. And my girl would get off on that shit. I've learned she'll let me fuck her in the Blue Box sometimes. She likes knowing people are watching and masturbating to us having sex. My girl is a dirty fucking freak like me. We're a match made in kinky hell.

"I love when you wear shit like this," I tell Nat against her ear, sliding a hand up her black dress to where her breasts are. The V-neck dips low and I boldly slide my hand under the material to access her tit. "Your hoodies don't let me touch your tits in front of everyone."

She moans, rubbing her ass against me. "Do you think anyone would notice if you lifted my dress and fucked me right here."

I pinch her nipple and nip at her ear. "Bad girl. Teasing for things that can't happen. But if you're a good girl and let me do my job, I'll fuck you in the bathroom right after this."

"Men's or women's restroom?"

"Men's."

"Oooh, that's hot," she says. "What if they try to touch?"

"I'll fucking rip their arms off and beat them with them."

She laughs as I slide my hand out of her dress. The grumpy bar owner walks onto the small stage over to the microphone.

"Good evening," the man says. "Tonight, as you all know, is Talent Night. And just like every Friday, my sister is going to kick things off." *Ahhh, sister. Not boyfriend.* He waggles his finger at the brunette. "No encores this time. We have drinks to make."

Her cheeks flame and the crowd chuckles. Several guys up front chant "encore" just to piss the bar owner off. As he stalks off the small stage, he grabs her bicep, speaking lowly to her. She bows her head and nods before breaking from his grip. As soon as she's in front of the microphone, her body relaxes.

She belongs in front of a crowd.

Not behind a bar beside her asshole brother.

Her brown hair has blue and purple feathers braided into some strands framing her face. Dark, black eyeliner, mascara, and eyeshadow hides her blue eyes from the world. Her plump lips are painted bright red. The whole look isn't exactly working for her. If she signs with us, I know Ronan won't like it. He'll want all the shit off so he can see her eyes. He always says you can reach the soul of a person—which when you're selling records, it's exactly what you want—by looking in their eyes. In reality, he just likes the innocent look. Fucking pervert. I don't give a fuck about her look. It's her voice I care about.

The music starts playing on the speakers and she begins singing. Her glittery navy-blue painted nails shimmer under the lights. As she belts out the words to a song I've never heard before, her breasts bounce and jiggle, threatening to spill from her top.

The slutty ensemble is distracting. Every note that spills past her red lips is beautiful and fucking poetic, yet looking at her cheapens her sound. I critique everything about her. Her stage presence is spot-on. She commands the crowd. Her voice is fucking flawless. It's her goddamn outfit and look that needs work. But she's a win. I'm going to sign her to Harose one way or another.

When the song is over, she shoots her gaze over to her brother as if to ask if she can do one more. He shakes his head sharply. Fucking asshole.

"Thank you," she murmurs to the crowd.

The loudmouths from the front chant "encore" over and over again, but she ignores them, heading back over to the bar. Soon, some toneless woman starts singing.

"Oh my God," Nat says, turning in my arms. "She's amazing. Are you going to sign her?"

I kiss her pouty lips. "I want to. Her brother

looks like a problem, though. A little too fucking controlling for my taste."

She beams at me. "You'll convince them. You always do. You have a great eye for finding talent."

"Are you buttering me up because you want me to fuck you, baby?" I tease, loving the flare of lust in her green eyes.

"Actually," she groans. "I was being genuine because I love you and you should know these things. About how wonderful you are."

I freeze for a moment, digesting her words. I've thought it for months, but I've never spoken it before. Neither has she.

"You love me?" I growl, searing her with my intense gaze.

Her lashes flutter as she smiles. "I've loved you for a long time, Ren."

"Fucking same, baby," I mutter, pressing my lips to hers. "I love you too."

"Now can we fuck in the bathroom?" she purrs, gripping my T-shirt in her fist.

My dick hardens as she starts to drag me away. Someone whistles at us, but we ignore them. I grab her wrist before hauling her out of the busy bar to the men's room. When we burst inside, two guys are using the urinals. One of the stalls is empty, so we push inside.

"Don't touch anything," I bark out. "You're to hold your dress up and let me do all the work, beautiful."

"Jesus," someone grumbles from nearby. "I'm trying to piss."

She giggles, making my dick throb in my jeans. I pull up her dress and she takes over, holding it at her hips. Sliding my finger along the crack of her ass, I seek out her cunt to see if she's ready for me. Just like always, my finger slides right inside of her. She's slick and dripping with arousal. I practically yank my dick out of my jeans and boxers, eager to be inside her. Gripping my dick in one hand while the other snakes around to her throat, I push against her and then slide into her heat. We both moan at the sensation.

The guy in the stall next to us groans. But it sounds sexual. Like hearing two people fuck while he takes a shit is enough to make his dick hard enough to whack off to.

I grip Nat's throat and press my mouth to her ear as I thrust my hips. "You're turning that guy on, baby. I think he likes the sexy sounds coming out of your mouth."

She whimpers. "Ren, oh God! Fuck me hard."

I bite her ear and laugh. "Dirty girl."

Soon, the people around us fade as I fuck my woman into oblivion. Her screams grow louder until she's coming all over my dick that's buried deep inside her. The fucking stall walls nearly come down around us. I grunt out my own release, loving the moan that escapes her. Sliding out of her, I smile, knowing my cum is going to run down her thighs for the next little while and there's not a damn thing she can do about it. I'm going to steal her panties too. She can spend the rest of the night rubbing her thighs together so all the other bar patrons will see just how much cum her boyfriend shot up inside of her.

"Ren?" she asks, breaking from my hold to turn and face me. She bends to grab her panties, but I hold out my hand for her to relinquish them. Her eyes roll, but she hands them over before letting her dress fall back into place. I pocket the panties and admire her pretty face that's flushed pink.

Goddamn, she's so fucking beautiful right after she comes.

"Yeah, baby?"

"Take me home. There are things I want you to do with me that we can't do here."

"Like what?"

"You know what." Her green eyes smolder at me.

Anal.

She's going to let me finally put it in her ass.

Grabbing a handful of her ass cheeks over her dress, I pull her to me, my still-wet dick smearing across the front of her black dress. "You craving a fat cock in your ass, beautiful?"

"Maybe," she purrs.

"You're a temptation I'll never be able to ignore," I tell her, kissing her on the lips.

Her mouth curls up into a wicked grin. "Good. You ever ignore this temptation and she'll tie you up and have her filthy way with you."

I shrug and laugh. "I don't know. The situation seems win-win if you ask me."

"You? Give up control to me? I'd love to see that," she snorts.

She's right. As hot as it would be with her naked and commanding me, I'd much rather truss her up and have my way with her.

"Let's get out of here," I tell her as I step back to pull up my boxers and jeans. "I have a pretty ass to ruin."

"What about the girl?" she asks, seeming to suddenly remember why we're here in the first place.

"She can wait. My girl, however, cannot."

"You're right," she muses. "I don't like to wait. I'm very impatient."

"And demanding," I supply.

"And perfect," she quips with a huff.

I grin at her. "And fucking perfect."

The way she looks at me as though I'm every star in her sky, it does something to me. Cements us in a way I never thought possible with a woman. She's my world too. The sun and the moon.

"Let's get out of here before I hire someone to marry us in this stall," I growl, grabbing her wrist.

Her smile is my undoing.

With a wink, I promise her the world.

One day soon she'll be forever mine.

I'll blow my brother's mind when I drag her down to the courthouse and give her my last name. But it's coming. You don't catch a beautiful girl by her throat and let her get away.

No, you keep her.

And you count every second you have with her.

One.

Two.

Three.

Breathe.

THE END

UP NEXT!

Daddy Me

A K&K Kinky Reads Collection

coming soon!

BOOKS

by

KER DUKEY
&
K WEBSTER

Pretty Stolen Dolls
Pretty Lost Dolls
Pretty New Doll
Pretty Broken Dolls

THE V *series* GAMES

Vlad

Ven

Vas

KKinky Reads Collection:

Share Me

Choke Me

Daddy Me

The Elite Seven Series:

Lust by Ker Dukey

Pride by J.D. Hollyfield

Wrath by Claire C. Riley

Envy by MN Forgy

Gluttony by K Webster

Sloth by Giana Darling

Greed by Ker Dukey and K Webster

THE
FOUR FATHERS
SERIES

Blackstone by J.D. Hollyfield

Kingston by Dani Rene

Pearson by K Webster

Wheeler by Ker Dukey

THE

FOUR SONS

SERIES

Nixon by Ker Dukey

Hayden by J.D. Hollfield

Brock by Dani Rene

Camden by K Webster

AKNOWLEDGEMENTS

thank you!

Thank you to our wonderful husbands. Baby Daddy and Mr. Webster are the real inspirations!

Ker and K would like to thank each other for being so amazing and beautiful and sweet and precious and funny and talented and hard working and...yeah, you get the point. (We love each other 1000%!)

A huge thank you to our reader groups. You all are insanely supportive and we can't thank you enough.

Thanks so much to Terrie Arasin and Misty Walker! Two of the best PAs everrrr! We love you ladies!

A gigantic thank you to those who always help K out. Elizabeth Clinton, Ella Stewart, Misty Walker,

Holly Sparks, Jillian Ruize, Gina Behrends, and Nikki Ash—you ladies are amazing!

Great thanks to Ker's awesome ladies for helping make this book is as awesome as can be! Couldn't have done it without you: Ashley Cestra, Rosa Saucedo, PA Allison, Teresa Nicholson.

A big thank you to our author friends who have given us your friendship and your support. You have no idea how much that means to us.

Thank you to all of our blogger friends both big and small that go above and beyond to always share our stuff. You all rock! #AllBlogsMatter

Emily A. Lawrence with Lawrence Editing, thank you SO much for editing this book. You rock!!

A big thanks to our PR gal, Nicole Blanchard. You are fabulous at what you do!

Lastly but certainly not least of all, thank you to all of the wonderful readers out there who are willing to hear our stories and enjoy the characters like we do. It means the world to us!

ABOUT KER DUKEY

My books all tend to be darker romance, the edge of your seat, angst-filled reads. My advice to my readers when starting one of my titles... prepare for the unexpected.

I have always had a passion for storytelling, whether it be through lyrics or bedtime stories with my sisters growing up.

My mom would always have a book in her hand when I was young and passed on her love for reading, inspiring me to venture into writing my own. Not all love stories are made from light- some are created in darkness but are just as powerful and worth telling.

When I'm not lost in the world of characters, I love spending time with my family. I'm a mom and that comes first in my life, but when I do get down time, I love attending music concerts or reading events with my younger sister.

Amazon author page:
Website: https://amzn.to/2W5cQ6a
Facebook: https://bit.ly/1RbsIKV
Twitter: https://bit.ly/1RZMzN2
Instagram http://bit.ly/2PoSaoz
BookBub http://bit.ly/2P5OSiy
Newsletter: http://eepurl.com/opJxT
Goodreads: http://bit.ly/2kuKWJl

Contact me here:

Ker: Kerryduke34@gmail.com
Ker's PA: terriesin@gmail.com

ABOUT AUTHOR K WEBSTER

K Webster is the *USA Today* bestselling author of over seventy-five romance books in many different genres including contemporary romance, historical romance, paranormal romance, dark romance, sci-fi romance, romantic suspense, taboo romance, and erotic romance. When not spending time with her hilarious and handsome husband and two adorable children, she's active on social media connecting with her readers.

Her other passions besides writing include reading and graphic design. K can always be found in front of her computer chasing her next idea and taking action. She looks forward to the day when she will see one of her titles on the big screen.

Join K Webster's newsletter to receive a couple

of updates a month on new releases and exclusive content. To join, all you need to do is go here.

Facebook

Blog

Twitter

Email

Goodreads

Instagram

Bookbub

K&K
KINKY READS

Made in the USA
Middletown, DE
29 March 2022